"This isn't wise," she muttered for Griff alone

"I want to talk to you," he told her softly. "Why else do you think I came to dinner at all?"

"Because you were asked," she snapped.

"Because I wanted to see you," he corrected in a low voice.

Sarah turned to him sharply, shaking her head at the warmth of his gaze. "Griff, I—"

"Do you realize that's the first time you've called me by my name?" he cut in gruffly.

Delicate color entered her cheeks. "This afternoon was a mistake—"

"No mistake, Sarah," he cut in firmly. "A little ill-timed, perhaps, but..."

CAROLE MORTIMER is the author of more than eighty top-selling romance novels. Her strong traditional stories with their distinctly modern appeal, fascinating characters and involving plots have earned her an enthusiastic audience worldwide. Carole Mortimer lives on the Isle of Man with her family and a menagerie of pets. She claims this busy household has helped to inspire her writing.

Books by Carole Mortimer

HARLEQUIN PRESENTS

Don't miss any of our special offers. Write to us at the following address for information on our newest releases.

Harlequin Reader Service
P.O. Box 1397, Buffalo, NY 14240
Canadian address: P.O. Box 603,
Fort Erie, Ont. L2A 5X3

Carole Mortimer

THE JILTED BRIDEGROOM

Harlequin Books

TORONTO • NEW YORK • LONDON
AMSTERDAM • PARIS • SYDNEY • HAMBURG
STOCKHOLM • ATHENS • TOKYO • MILAN
MADRID • WARSAW • BUDAPEST • AUCKLAND

My husband, Frank,
With all my love

Harlequin Presents Plus first edition June 1993
ISBN 0-373-11559-8

Original hardcover edition published in 1992
by Mills & Boon Limited

THE JILTED BRIDEGROOM

CHAPTER ONE

A MAN'S shirt lay in the hallway.

A pair of trousers along the passageway to the bedrooms.

A pair of black socks, one in the doorway of the spare bedroom, the second actually inside the bedroom.

And outside the door to the adjoining bathroom lay a pair of——

Sarah, who had followed this trail of clothing, looked up with a start of surprise as the door opened in front of her, her eyes widening still further as she took in the fact that the man standing in the doorway only had a towel draped about his hips to hide his nakedness, his dark hair still damp from the shower he had obviously just taken, although he looked as if he had been drying his tousled hair with another towel that now lay draped about his neck.

It was difficult not to stare at him, his body deeply tanned, dark hair growing across his broad chest and down beneath the towel, his shoulders wide, his body tapering to his tautly muscled stomach, the dark hair on his legs clinging damply to his skin where he hadn't taken the time to dry himself properly.

Sarah's gaze returned quickly to the grimness of his face, an incredibly handsome face, despite his obvious displeasure and puzzlement at finding her here.

She wasn't too happy about being here herself—but that was another story!

It was a ruggedly hewn face, his tawny-coloured eyes having a knowledge in them that spoke plainly of cynicism towards a life that had been seen and experienced rather than just read about. His nose was long and straight, laughter lines beside those incredible eyes and the sensuality of his mouth. Although the mouth wasn't smiling now, and his chin, with that intriguing cleft in its centre, was set at an arrogant angle.

'Who are you?' she demanded in English—because her French was non-existent!—infusing much more bravado into her voice than she actually felt. Who *was* he?

'Never mind who I am.' He was as English as she was! 'What do you think you're doing in here?'

What was *she* doing here? This was Virginia Major's villa in the tiny village of Aribeau in the south of France, a sprawling one-storey building, the comfortable lounge, kitchen, and three bedrooms all surrounding the small courtyard, baskets of sweet-smelling flowers adorning the wooden beams out there, the lounge itself overlooking the private swimming-pool and landscaped garden.

And, as far as Sarah was aware, there should be no one else here just now, Virginia Major having left several days earlier, stopping over briefly in London during the weekend, for her brother's wedding, before going on to Southampton to join a cruise ship.

The man standing in front of her looked about them with narrowed eyes at her continued lack of response. 'I can't see that anything is missing,' he sighed. 'But perhaps you had better empty out your pockets anyway, just in case.' He looked irritated by the situation—as he saw it!

And as Sarah now realised he saw it! '*I'm* not a burglar!' she defended indignantly; if anyone could be called an intruder here it was *him*!

'No?' he derided tauntingly, his expression one of scepticism. 'I can't think of any other reason for your being in the villa.'

'Can't you indeed?' she bit out angrily.

She was resentful enough of being here without having to deal with intruders who acted as if they owned the place. And she knew he didn't do that; it was because the widowed Virginia Major had no one else to ask that Clarissa had volunteered Sarah in the first place!

'And just what do you think this is?' she challenged, holding up the brightly coloured watering-can she had been clutching in her hand during the whole conversation.

Dark brows rose. 'A weapon?' he suggested derisively.

'A plastic watering-can!' Sarah scorned disbelievingly.

'Hm, perhaps not a weapon. At least,' he added mockingly, 'not one that's likely to be very effective.'

Not against a man who looked as powerful as he did, anyway, she conceded impatiently. 'I told you, I'm not a burglar,' she snapped irritably, her eyes flashing deeply green.

Really, she had just wanted to get the job over and done with and get out; this man was just delaying her.

'Then what are you doing walking around the house with it?' He still looked suspicious of her motives.

Sarah sighed her impatience, sure she shouldn't be the one on the receiving end of the questioning. As far as she was aware, she had the only key to the villa in her shorts pocket, entrusted to her by Virginia Major while she was away.

But this man had to have got in somehow, and she hadn't seen any signs of a forced entry when she'd let herself in earlier.

Because of that she had to accept the fact that he might have obtained a key from someone, and if he did happen to be a friend of Mrs Major's she could hardly order him out of the place. Although if he refused there was no way she could make him leave anyway, he was so much bigger than her.

'Well?' he prompted at her lengthy silence, somehow, even dressed in only a towel as he was, managing to look very tall and powerful.

She gave him a disparaging look. 'Aren't you getting cold, dressed like that?' She felt uncomfortable carrying on a conversation with a complete stranger who was almost naked, even if he didn't seem in the least bothered by the fact himself.

His mouth quirked at her obvious unease. 'Not in the least.' His stance was deliberately provocative, almost challenging, the towel slipping even further down his hips. 'Is it bothering you?' He raised mocking brows.

'Not in the least,' she echoed coldly. She had seen enough half-dressed men during the last week; it was just that she was alone with this one, and he, as far as she could tell, was wearing only that loosely draped towel!

He shrugged. 'You still haven't answered my question as to just what you're doing here,' he reminded softly.

'I would have thought this spoke for itself.' Once again she indicated the watering-can she still held, annoyed to see that her hand was shaking slightly at the unexpected encounter with this arrogant man.

'Oh, it does.' He strolled further into the bedroom, having all the grace of movement of a feline. 'It tells me you have a fetish for plastic watering-cans!' He was standing very close now, close enough for Sarah to smell the cleanness of his body and the slightly elusive cologne he had rubbed into his flesh.

Sarah took an instinctive step backwards, unconcerned with how cowardly the movement must look to him. She was only five feet two inches in height—barely reached the man's shoulders—very slender in close-fitting shorts and a loose green shirt, her face bare of make-up in the hot May sun, her long blonde hair having been bleached even blonder by the hours she had spent out in that sun, secured at her crown with a green ribbon at the moment for coolness.

The totally male assessment of her appearance in this man's golden-coloured eyes as he looked at her made her wish she weren't dressed with the casualness of a teenager; at twenty-three, she was far from being that!

And yet what else should she have worn on a hot day in this picturesque village in the south of France?

'It tells you...' Her impatience was directed as much at herself as it was at him, impatience because she could possibly care what this dangerous-looking stranger thought of her appearance.

Dangerous?

Yes, he was, she acknowledged slowly. But not in a violent way. There was an air of power about him, a coldness in his eyes occasionally that spoke of cruelty if necessary. And something about the very look of him told her that sometimes he deemed it very necessary.

'It *should* tell you,' she amended pointedly, 'that I'm here to water the plants.'

And she wasn't exactly pleased about having to do it! She had come on holiday with Clarissa and her family as a favour to the other woman, and ended up being lent out to water Virginia Major's plants as if she were a servant.

'Hm.' The man in front of her nodded thoughtfully, as if the idea had crossed his mind before now. 'Why?' He shot the question at her.

It was the question she had been asking herself the last five days! Virginia Major was Clarissa's acquaintance, not hers, and yet Clarissa had felt no compunction about offering her services as plant-waterer. Admittedly she was here with the family on a working holiday, but she had done that more as a favour to her mother's friend than out of any real desire to come away with the Forbes family. She certainly hadn't expected to be loaned out to a neighbour Clarissa had got to know only briefly. But Clarissa certainly had no intention of doing this menial job herself, despite being the one to make the offer in the first place!

'So that the plants don't die, of course.' She answered the man snappily again, not exactly angry with him, but if he wanted to ask silly questions he was the one who was going to get the sharp edge of her tongue.

'Ah,' he nodded again, without conviction, 'I see.'

Sarah gave a derisive sigh. 'Do you?'

'No,' he admitted ruefully, looking for all the world like a puzzled little boy.

She pursed her mouth impatiently, not at all fooled by his expression; this man was sharply intelligent, she had no doubt of that. 'It's quite simple really,' she said with an implied sarcasm. 'While Mrs Major is away I come in to check that the villa hasn't been broken in to, and to water whatever plants I feel are in need of it.'

'It's very good of you to do that for Virginia,' he said admiringly.

'Not really,' Sarah told him drily.

He arched dark brows. 'No?'

'No,' she smiled wryly. Clarissa had got to know their English neighbour only briefly before the other woman flew to England. It was ironic really; they had all travelled over here to spend a month in the south of France, and Virginia Major had left the permanent home she had here a few days later to join a cruise ship that was travelling around the Caribbean Islands.

At least, Clarissa and Roger and their three children—Ben, eighteen, Sally, sixteen, and Stephen, nine—were here on holiday; Sarah had been asked along to help out Clarissa, who had recently been in hospital for a minor operation and felt she couldn't cope with the care of Stephen on her own, mainly. This was Sarah's own holiday from her nursing job, but as she hadn't actually been intending to go away anywhere, and, as a favour to her mother, she had agreed to accompany the Forbes family to France.

Not having lived at home with her mother for some years, she had known the Forbes family only vaguely. She had certainly got to know all of them better over the last ten days, wished she had stayed at home to do the decorating in her flat she had originally intended to fill her holiday time!

She had done nothing but run around after one member of the family or another since their arrival here. She had certainly ended up doing much more than helping out with young Stephen. It had been adding insult to injury when Clarissa had calmly offered Sarah's services as housekeeper for Virginia Major because the other woman had given her own maid the same three weeks' holiday as herself, having forgotten all about her plants' needing watering!

And at only her second visit here she had walked into goodness knew what sort of a situation. But this man's use, minutes ago, of Mrs Major's first name at least confirmed he knew her well enough for that. Unless she had inadvertently used it herself? No, she was sure she hadn't, not friendly with the other woman enough herself to be so familiar. And there was the fact that he was English too—that had to be more than coincidence.

'I'm staying in the neighbouring villa you can see slightly down the hillside,' she supplied irritably, wishing she knew exactly what was going on.

He moved to the window, the towel slipping precariously as he leant forward to look out at the roof of the pink and cream villa that could just be seen through the trees.

He turned back to her, grinning rakishly as he retrieved the towel before it could fall off him completely. 'Another of the idle rich, hm?' he taunted.

Her mouth twisted. 'The family I'm here working for may be,' she bit out, 'but I'm certainly not. I'm here to look after their nine-year-old son Stephen.' But she had also become chief cook and bottle-washer since arriving here! The Forbeses hadn't needed a temporary nanny for Stephen—they had needed a cook and a maid as well. And she seemed to fit the description! She had already decided she would never be swayed by family affection and help out so-called friends of her mother again.

'So you're a sort of nanny, Miss...?' He looked at her enquiringly.

'Williams,' she supplied abruptly. 'Sarah Williams. And I'm not a sort of anything, I'm actually a trained nurse on holiday. Or, at least, supposedly so,' she added drily. 'I've answered your questions; now perhaps you could answer a few of mine.' She made no move to go through to the rest of the villa, even though there were no more plants to be watered in this room.

She was very much aware of the pre-cariousness of her position alone in the villa with an almost naked man, but she felt she would be better standing her ground rather than making a move of any sort, particularly one that could look in the least nervous.

'Who are *you*?' She looked at him challeng-ingly. 'And what are you doing here?'

'My name is Griff Morgan.' He held out his hand to her politely, incongruously so in the circumstances. 'It's Griffin really, but even people who aren't my friends call me Griff,' he added with a mischievous grin. 'Virginia calls me Griff,' he added cajolingly.

Sarah took the proffered hand automati-cally, so disconcerted now that she didn't even notice when he forgot to let go of her hand again.

She frowned her puzzlement. 'Mrs Major didn't mention that anyone was coming to stay at the villa while she was away. In fact,' she shrugged, 'that's the reason I was asked to come here, because there was no one else.'

Griff smiled, the tawny-coloured eyes warm as his gaze swept across the golden loveliness of her face. 'That's because Virginia didn't know I was going to be here. I didn't know it myself until yesterday.' He grimaced.

Sarah looked at him curiously. 'What happened yesterday?'

He gave a derisive shrug. 'I felt in need of a break,' he dismissed lightly.

'But—Griff Morgan!' Her eyes had widened with sudden recognition of the name. 'You're the investigative reporter, aren't you?' she realised incredulously.

Most people, in England at least, had heard of the name Griff Morgan; he had made a career out of the type of exposé stories that the general public couldn't help but notice, sparing that public none of the graphic details.

Yes, Griff Morgan knew of all the hell life had to offer, had seen most of it first-hand. Which probably accounted for that air of cynicism she had sensed about him on such brief acquaintance. And yet he seemed to have maintained his sense of humour too, those laughter lines about his eyes and mouth not a figment of her imagination.

'That's me,' he confirmed lightly, dismissing the idea of any importance being attached to that.

'I read the stories on drug addiction you did last year.' She shuddered at the memory. 'They were harrowing!'

Something of the horror flickered in his own eyes, and then disappeared, the amusement instantly back in his expression. 'They were meant to be,' he said dismissively. 'And the answer to the second question you asked me a minute ago is that, for the moment, I'm staying here.'

Sarah frowned at this knowledge. 'When you say "staying here" do you mean——?'

'I mean,' Griff Morgan took up her hesitant speech, 'that until I decide otherwise I'm going to live at the villa. I always stay here when I can get away,' he added with a shrug as she still didn't look convinced. Griff looked amused—at her expense! 'I'm sure that once Virginia gets back from her cruise she'll confirm all this for you. In the meantime——'

'In the meantime I think you should let go of my hand!' She extricated herself with difficulty, having suddenly become aware of a lightly caressing thumb against her palm, the intimacy of the action not lost on her. 'I really do have to finish watering these plants,' she added, slightly agitated, a delicate blush to her cheeks.

He strolled across the bedroom to sort through the crumpled clothes that lay in the open suitcase on the floor. 'I just fell into bed when I arrived last night,' he ruefully explained the untidiness. 'I was a little tired. No—make that exhausted,' he grimaced.

'Have you been working on another story?' She found it difficult to keep the avid interest out of her voice, intrigued in spite of herself.

Besides, it helped take her mind off the rumpled intimacy of the bed behind him, the indentation his head had left on the pillow still there from when he had got out of bed earlier.

'Something like that,' he said drily.

'They said that when you did the drug-addiction stories last year you actually took drugs yourself.' She frowned at the danger of that much dedication, important as it was to expose the people who pushed and sold those drugs.

'Never!' he denied harshly, making a visible effort to regain his composure as he realised he had briefly lost it. 'I wouldn't get involved in that destruction for any price. No, Sarah,' he shook his head, 'I just gave a good impression of being involved. I was lucky enough to get away with it. Most of the people in that business play dirty.' He frowned, the humour he made such an effort to maintain once again pushed aside in favour of a stronger emotion, anger this time. 'Very dirty,' he added grimly.

'Is it worth risking your life just to get a story?' She shook her head.

His mouth quirked, the warmth back in his eyes, making Sarah wonder if she had imagined the cold anger in his face a moment ago. Looking at him now, lazily relaxed, it was hard to imagine him being anything else. He looked like a man who enjoyed life to the full.

He tapped her lightly on the end of her nose with one long, tapered finger. 'All of life is a gamble, little one,' he drawled. 'And if I didn't achieve more than getting a story for all that effort maybe it wouldn't be worth it,' he added seriously. 'But if it means just one of those ba— one pusher,' he amended tautly, 'can be put behind bars then that's reason enough for me to take the risk. I can't believe that you, as a nurse, don't have a similar opinion,' he cajoled.

She did. Of course she did. But, 'I don't risk my own life trying to do something about it.'

'You can't seem to make up your mind whether that's a good thing or a bad thing,' he said teasingly. 'Let's forget about all that,' he dismissed firmly. 'And you can answer me a question that's been puzzling me ever since I got here.'

Sarah couldn't look away from the warmth of those tawny-coloured eyes, mesmerised by their depths, held captive by the deep gold flecks within the light brown. 'Yes?' she prompted huskily.

He grinned, the cleft looking twice as endearing. 'Where the hell is Jasper?' His mouth quirked with humour. 'I haven't seen the little devil since I arrived.'

Sarah gave him a slightly scathing look for the frivolousness of the question after they had been talking so seriously. But then, maybe this was his answer to not being completely destroyed by the horrors of life that he wrote about. As a nurse, she too had to deal with life or death situations which, if she'd allowed herself to become too emotionally involved, could have driven her completely insane.

'Mrs Major felt it would be better if her cat went to board at his usual place while she was away,' she dismissed, just glad that Clarissa hadn't volunteered her to look after the damned cat too! 'Apparently, he needs a lot of care, and——'

'Virginia has created a monster,' he acknowledged. 'It comes of not having any children, I believe.'

'I wouldn't know about that.' Sarah was deliberately evasive, not wishing to get into a discussion about the other woman's private life with a man who was, at least to her, a complete stranger. Even if he did seem to know Virginia Major and her lifestyle very well.

It was in *what* capacity he knew the other woman that kept niggling away at her.

She gave him a searching look, seeing past the humour and charm to the rugged leanness of his body, the sensual knowledge in his eyes. In his mid-thirties, there was no doubting that he was devastatingly attractive.

But just where did Virginia Major fit into his life? Or, rather, he into hers, as he appeared to be the one who was a guest in her villa?

The other woman was older than him by at least ten years, possibly as many as fifteen. But she was still a beautiful woman, had a sexily voluptuous figure that showed to advantage in the fashionably flattering clothes she always wore, her hair still silkily blonde, her face youthfully beautiful with the aid of expertly applied make-up.

Sarah knew little or nothing about the other woman's personal life, and she knew that much to her chagrin, Clarissa hadn't been able to find out a lot about her private life either. Not that she hadn't tried!

Sarah wasn't too proud of the suspicions she now had concerning the relationship between Griff Morgan and Virginia Major, but she couldn't help wondering if the reason the other woman had kept so much to herself while living here was because she preferred the friends she had made while living in England—one very special 'friend' in particular. Goodness knew, Virginia Major would be far from the first woman to make a fool of herself over some unsuitable man. Who knew that better than Sarah herself?

Tawny-coloured eyes were narrowed on her as she looked up at Griff, his expression questioning. 'Is there something wrong?' He frowned.

'Nothing at all,' she denied briskly, breaking his gaze abruptly. 'I really must finish up here and be on my way; I promised Stephen that I would take him swimming before lunch.' And there was likely to be a temper tantrum if she didn't keep her word. Of the three children

Stephen was most like his mother, given to venting his temper if he didn't get his own way.

Living in such close contact with Clarissa these last ten days had certainly given Sarah a new insight into the woman who had always seemed so beautiful and charming on the few occasions she had been visiting Sarah's mother at the same time as Sarah herself.

'Look, if you would like to finish watering the plants while I throw on some clothes,' Griff suggested briskly, 'we can carry on talking over a cup of coffee.'

'And how would—your friend, Mrs Major, feel about that?' Sarah voiced her thoughts about that relationship, having no intention of becoming a bone of contention between the two over the simple sharing of a cup of coffee!

'Virginia?' He sounded surprised that she should even come into consideration over the casual suggestion. 'She wouldn't mind your having Ah,' he nodded slowly as her meaning sank in. 'My *friend* Virginia,' he repeated in amusement. 'Well, I really don't think she could object to my offering you a cup of coffee. And I've never known her to be the possessive type.' He looked Sarah over speculatively. 'So if you're lonely during your stay here ...'

Sarah's cheeks became flushed at the innuendo. 'Just because *you're* having an affair with a woman almost old enough to be your mother is no reason to think you can insult me!' she bit out scornfully.

'I wasn't insulting you, Sarah,' he mocked. 'Far from it. Some women would have seen my suggestion as a compliment.'

'Well, I'm not one of them!' She shuddered at the thought of it; out of the frying-pan into the fire!

'Obviously,' he drawled derisively. 'And I'm sure Virginia wouldn't appreciate that remark you made about her being almost old enough to be my mother; she's only in her forties.'

'Still far too old for you,' Sarah maintained stiffly.

'I believe she might prefer to be called experienced rather than old,' Griff taunted. 'And don't mock the fact that I stay here often between stories; my name may be known worldwide, all my expenses paid by my newspaper, but reporters themselves don't actually earn that much money, and when I'm not working I like to enjoy life.' He shrugged. 'As you can see, by this villa, the pool out back, Virginia is rich enough to ensure that I do that.'

Sarah looked at him with distaste as his meaning became clear. 'And in return for providing all this luxury she gets you,' she said with contempt. 'I never imagined Griff Morgan as no more than a kept man!'

'Well, now you know,' he mocked.

'Now I know,' she echoed with disgust. 'I think I had better be going.' She turned to leave, totally disillusioned with the way this incredibly talented man chose to live. 'I can finish watering the rest of the plants tomorrow.' When he wouldn't be here, she hoped!

'Yes—you mustn't keep Stephen waiting,' he derided softly, following her out to the hallway. 'I'd rather be answerable to a beautiful woman like Virginia than a spoilt child,' he softly mocked her.

'Then that's where we differ.' She turned to glare at him as she reached the door, her head tilted back as he stood too close to her, the dark hair completely dry now, curling softly over his forehead and ears. 'I only have another two and a half weeks of this to put up with, and then I'm never going to be answerable to this particular spoilt child again.' She was only seeing it through this time because she knew her mother would never forgive her if she supposedly let down her good friend Clarissa. Sarah's own sense of family loyalty was enough to make her see through what was turning into a hellish holiday.

She shook her head impatiently at Griff Morgan. 'I never would have believed this of you. All of your articles have dealt with a freedom of some kind, and now it turns out you're no better than a—a gigolo yourself!' Her eyes were full of the disillusionment she had suffered through this knowledge. This man had always seemed to represent a certain truth, a freedom, and yet he sold his own principles for a life of comfort and physical indulgence whenever he required it.

'I am?' He seemed amused at the prospect. 'Maybe I should do a story based on that very subject.'

Her eyes flashed her disgust. 'You certainly wouldn't have to go very far for the research!'

She was still shaking with anger by the time she got into the hire-car Clarissa and Roger let her use to drive over here, colour darkening her cheeks as she turned from reversing down the driveway to find Griffin Morgan watching her from the open doorway of the villa, completely unconcerned by the fact that he still only wore a towel draped about his hips to hide his naked-ness!

She dragged her gaze away with effort, un-able to deny his undoubted attraction, despite knowing what she now did about his personal life.

Unfortunately, much as she tried, she couldn't shake the man from her thoughts for the rest of the day. She had never met anyone quite like him before, and she found herself in-dulging in thoughts of him at the most inop-portune moments, only giving half her usual attention to Stephen, a fact he took full advan-tage of by being more unruly than normal, cul-minating in his pushing a newly oiled Sally into the pool, the water a cool shock to her skin. Her outraged screams woke Clarissa up as she slept on one of the loungers beside the pool, and even the easygoing Roger looked irritated by the commotion as he rushed from inside the villa to see what all the noise was about.

Sally created such a fuss that Sarah was left feeling the one responsible for the whole inci-dent, Stephen gently but indulgently scolded by his mother for his 'teasing'!

'Just ignore Sally,' Ben advised as Sarah pre-pared a salad for dinner, her movements controlled as she did her best to hold on to her own temper—and her tongue!

Ignore that spoilt little madam! Sarah knew what she would like to do with the young girl—with the whole family, in fact.

Of them all Ben was undoubtedly the nicest, often taking pity on her and helping her out with the numerous jobs that seemed to be included under the liberal title Clarissa had given her of 'family help'.

Sarah knew she wouldn't have got herself into this situation at all if she hadn't thought a break away from England was exactly what she needed right now. Not 'what the doctor ordered' certainly; Simon had been furious at her plans to go to France for a month, but it had been his very anger that had given her the impetus to accept Clarissa's offer in the first place.

He had a lot to answer for!

It was almost nine o'clock that evening before she really had a chance to sit down and relax, indulging herself with the English newspapers that had been purchased that morning. They were one day old, but this reminder of home, of a promised end to this so-called 'working holiday', was another one of the things that kept her from telling Clarissa what she thought of her and her spoilt family.

Sarah gave an inward gasp at the picture of Griff with a smilingly lovely woman at his side on the third page of the first newspaper she opened. The story that accompanied the photograph made her gasp even more.

Saturday should have been Griff Morgan's wedding-day!

CHAPTER TWO

THE woman standing at Griff's side in the photograph was his fiancée, Sandra Preston, the daughter of the owner of the group of newspapers Griff worked for. Griff had waited at the altar for his bride for almost an hour, finally having to accept that she had no intention of arriving.

My God, no wonder he had seemed so cynical and—and yes, slightly reckless today. Sarah wasn't to have known it at the time, but that cynicism, at least part of it, obviously came from the recent hurt he had suffered at the hands of his fiancée, and in such a humiliating way.

How could any woman leave a man standing at the altar in that way, knowing she had no intention of joining him there?

It said in the newspaper article that Sandra Preston had gone off to the family home in the Bahamas to 'get away for a while and think', and the reporter wondered where the jilted bridegroom had disappeared to. In fact, the headline of the story was, 'Where are you, Griff?'

Sarah knew exactly where the jilted bridegroom was. He was staying at the villa of another woman, a beautiful older woman who—Bridegroom...wedding...? Virginia Major had gone to London to attend her *brother's* wedding!

Oh, dear God, Griff Morgan had to be that brother; it would be too much of a coincidence for it to be any other way.

Not that Sarah could exactly blame him for letting her go on assuming the couple were lovers rather than siblings; she had made that conclusion on only a few minutes' acquaintance, and, after Griff's recent disillusionment, he must have just decided it was yet another kick in the teeth from a woman.

It was no good telling herself it wouldn't have happened at all if she hadn't been feeling so angry and frustrated by all the Forbes family. There was no excuse for the things she had said to Griff, for the assumption she had made; she had just been taking out her bad temper on him.

He must have been angry himself after the hurt and humiliation he had so recently been put through.

She put the newspaper down and stood up. 'I—I think I'll just go out for a stroll,' she announced to no one in particular, knowing that each member of this family was so self-engrossed that it wouldn't matter to any of them what she did—as long as none of them wanted something doing in her absence!

Clarissa looked up from the magazine she had been flicking through, a tall leggy redhead, still very beautiful, despite being in her early forties. 'Don't be ridiculous, Sarah,' she dismissed scathingly. 'You'll get eaten alive by the bugs out there!'

'Oh, but——'

'Besides,' the other woman added firmly, 'Roger and I are going down to Cannes shortly, so I'll need you to stay here with the children.'

There were the usual protests at being called a child from Ben and Sally.

Sarah felt like protesting herself. She had spent almost every evening of their stay with the children while Clarissa and Roger went off to one night-spot or another. The couple usually arrived back in the early hours of the morning, and then spent the following day sleeping it off in the sunshine.

Roger himself gave a groan of protest at this proposal, a much less social person, but the protest was quickly talked down by his much more dominating wife.

Sarah knew she might as well give up any idea of going for a walk tonight.

'Never mind, Sarah,' Ben grinned at her, as darkly good-looking as his company-director father, but with more of his mother's vivacity for life, 'you can beat us at dominoes if you like!'

That was the extent of her own night-life on this holiday!

But she gave a weary nod of acceptance as Sally flounced off to her bedroom after requesting to go into Cannes with her parents and being firmly refused.

Loud music soon blared out from her bedroom, and Sarah gave an inward plea for it not to wake Stephen—he would be awake half the night once he was disturbed. And, consequently, so would she!

But her mind was far from on the game of dominoes, the subject of Griff Morgan uppermost in her thoughts. She felt so awful about the way she had behaved with him now. And what sort of woman was Sandra Preston to do such a thing to him?

'Don't wait up for us, Sarah,' Clarissa told her coyly when she emerged from changing a short time later, her black dress clinging to her revealingly, her hair loose about her shoulders, her make-up heavier than she wore during the day. 'We expect to be late!' she added suggestively, clinging to Roger's arm as the couple left the villa.

No, Sarah frowned, she refused to believe there *could* be another woman like Clarissa. And yet Sandra Preston's behaviour seemed vaguely familiar in its selfishness . . .

She couldn't escape thoughts of Griff Morgan the next day either, wishing the time away until she could go over to the neighbouring villa, but knowing she would have to see the Forbes family settled in relative peace about the pool before excusing herself to go to the Major villa and water the plants.

It seemed a little out of place to use the key Mrs Major had left for her now; if Griff Morgan was still here—and she sincerely hoped he was!—then it could be a little awkward for both of them if she just walked in on him as she had the last time.

This time he might not even have got to the stage of wrapping the towel about his waist!

Sarah decided it might be wiser—and safer!— to knock on the door and wait to see if he answered it, moving restlessly on the doorstep as she waited for a response to her knock.

There wasn't one, and her disappointment was acute as she dejectedly let herself in with her key, coming to a startled halt as Griffin Morgan walked down the hallway towards her, wearing only a pair of bathing trunks this time!

'Come in, Sarah Williams,' he invited huskily, as she still stood in the doorway. 'I've been expecting you.'

She swallowed hard, watching dazedly as he walked past her, the slight thud of the door closing behind her somehow seeming final—and irrevocable.

'Sorry I didn't answer the door when you knocked.' He moved to stand in front of her now. 'I was lounging by the pool, and by the time I had realised it was actually someone knocking at the door you had already let yourself in.'

'I'm sorry about that. I—I still have the key.' She held it up for him to see, very conscious of the lean length of his body in the hip-hugging black bathing trunks, a gold medallion of St Christopher nestling in the dark hair on his chest today—and how apt that was, considering the amount of travelling around the world this man did. 'Perhaps I should give you the key back while you're staying here,' she suggested abruptly. 'I really shouldn't have just walked in here this morning, uninvited.'

Griff smiled as he moved his hand dismissively, his eyes the colour of warm golden honey, a strange contrast to his dark hair and tanned skin. 'You thought I was out,' he excused. 'Besides, I quite like having you just walk in. Do you realise you're the first person I've seen, apart from the gardener, since I arrived here two days ago? And his conversation is limited,' he added with a grimace. 'I'm sure my French isn't that bad!'

Sarah smiled. 'He's actually a little deaf.'

Griff's expression cleared. 'And I thought he was ignoring me!' He gave a soft laugh. 'I'll have to remember to talk louder the next time I see him.'

She nodded. 'He's really very nice.'

He quirked dark brows. 'How about the coffee we didn't manage the last time you were here?'

'I——'

'Don't refuse, Sarah,' he cut in quickly. 'I've been waiting for you to arrive all morning. I've already thrown away two pots of coffee that became stewed because I wasn't sure what time you would arrive today. Come on, Sarah, take pity on a fellow Brit, and accept,' he encouraged huskily.

She was very much aware that it was loneliness that motivated the invitation, but nevertheless, when he put it like this, it was heady stuff. And there lay the danger.

'Just to show you've forgiven me for yesterday,' he added persuasively.

Her eyes widened at this. 'That *I've* forgiven you? But you didn't do anything. I was the one who was offhand and pompous. I should never——'

'Offhand *and* pompous?' Griff mocked lightly. 'My, you are on a guilt trip, aren't you? So you found out about my fiasco of a wedding-day——'

'It was in all the English newspapers,' she sympathised.

'Finding out about that mess changes nothing.' He gave a dismissive shrug of his shoulders. 'I'm still the same person you were disgusted by yesterday.'

Sarah looked at him reprovingly. 'Virginia Major is your *sister*.'

'Ah, so you realised that too, did you?' He nodded appreciatively. 'Knowing my snobbish sister as I do, I don't think she would have been too thrilled by that other assumption you made about our relationship. Virginia is a great one for keeping up appearances,' he added derisively. 'Would have been scandalised that anyone could possibly think she would be involved in an affair. And especially one with a younger man!' he drawled.

Sarah groaned. 'I already feel badly enough about that!'

'Then let's not discuss my dear sister any further,' he dismissed easily. 'Why don't you go and water her plants while I pour us both some coffee? We mustn't let the plants fade away and die or she'll blame me for that too; I've already upset her enough by being left at the altar. She just may "never recover from the embarrassment of it all".' He grimaced ruefully as he mimicked the haughty tones of his older sister.

But from the little Sarah had come to know of the other woman, before she'd left for England, she wasn't at all surprised that this was her attitude over Griff's being jilted in the way he had. He was making very light of his own humiliation, probably because to dwell on it would be far too painful. No one could come away from an experience like that unscathed, and from the depth and emotion of Griff's newspaper articles it was easy to tell he was a sensitive person.

'Black, with one sugar,' she told him lightly. 'The coffee,' she prompted as he instantly looked puzzled.

He gave a self-derisive laugh. 'I thought it must be some type of food for the plants!'

'Perhaps it is,' Sarah derided, deciding to follow his lead and treat this second meeting as lightly as he seemed to want to. But no matter how he dismissed it she knew Sandra Preston's treatment of him had affected him deeply—as it would any man! She could see that by the strain about his eyes when he wasn't smiling that mischievous grin. 'But I'm not about to try it!' She gave a rueful laugh, following him through to the kitchen, filling up the brightly coloured watering-can before leaving him to pour the coffee.

The casual untidiness she had noticed in his bedroom yesterday seemed to have affected the rest of the villa today, things lying about haphazardly in every room, only Virginia Major's bedroom remaining exempt from the clutter. Now that she was aware of his real relationship to the other woman this perhaps wasn't so surprising! If she had actually bothered to think yesterday she would have realised that if he were Virginia Major's lover, as she had assumed he was, he would have been sharing the other woman's bedroom. Being sensible after the event wasn't really a lot of help to either of them!

Despite being siblings, Virginia Major and Griff Morgan were complete opposites, to look at and by nature. Virginia Major had a deep reserve about her, was extremely fastidious in all that she did, seeming to feel that everything had a place, and that it should be kept there. Griff was more open—probably considered that life was too short to be anything else—and his untidiness was all too obvious. Virginia was as tall as her brother, but instead of being dark like Griff she was a golden blonde, with slightly calculating blue eyes. Maybe, after all, Sarah could be forgiven for making such a wrong assumption about them!

She hummed softly to herself as she moved about the main bedroom, feeling a little more relaxed now that the initial awkwardness of seeing and talking to Griff again had passed. She accepted that he preferred to make light of the whole incident, because to dwell on it would only result in his having to go into further detail about Saturday, and he——

She let out a terrified scream as she heard something hiss down near her feet, too terrified even to look down, just in case it was something horrific.

Oh, God...! Griff Morgan had been to some exotic locations during his career—lord knew what it was that had made that hissing noise. Although her imagination was running wild.

'I heard you cry out.' A worried-looking Griff came hurrying into the room, still holding the sugar bowl in his hand where he had rushed straight from the kitchen after hearing her scream. 'What happened?' His sharp-eyed gaze moved quickly but methodically about the room, returning to her with a puzzled frown when he could find nothing there that could have caused her obvious distress. 'Sarah?' he prompted in a puzzled voice.

She was still frozen to the spot, too frightened to move. 'I—it's down there,' she told him through stiff lips, so tense that she couldn't even nod her head in the direction of the floor.

Griff gave her a look that clearly doubted her sanity, although his barely perceptible shrug seemed to imply he was perfectly willing to humour her, for the moment at least. 'What is?' he prompted cajolingly.

His condescending tone made her eyes flash deeply green. 'How should I know?' she snapped fiercely. 'I was just watering the plants near the bed here when I heard something *hissing*!'

Griff looked at her silently for several seconds before pursing his lips thoughtfully. 'But you...didn't see what...hissed at you?' His expression was bland.

'No,' she confirmed shakily. 'Don't just stand there.' Her body was so tense now that she felt as if she might snap. 'Do something!'

'Hold this, will you?' He placed the sugar bowl into one of her shaking hands. 'Perhaps it went under Virginia's bed.' He went down on his hands and knees, lifting up the frilled ruffle to look underneath. 'Yes, there he is.' He nodded his satisfaction, sitting back on his heels to look at the long bare length of Sarah's legs, making her very conscious of the brief cut of her green shorts, her bare feet thrust into white sandals. 'You weren't bitten?' He frowned up at her.

'No,' she shook her head tautly. 'I—is it . . . poisonous?'

'No,' Griff assured her. 'But you're sure your skin wasn't broken?'

Oh, God, what was *wrong*? 'No, it didn't actually touch me,' she explained tightly.

'Good.' He nodded his satisfaction. 'Not that I think Jasper has rabies,' he dismissed. 'But I wouldn't want to take the risk with you.' He lifted the pink ruffle about the base of the bed again. 'Come on out, Jasper,' he persuaded. 'Come on, no one is going to hurt you.'

Jasper? She had been frightened of a *cat*?

Griff picked up the metal-grey-coloured cat as he strode haughtily out from under the bed, looking for all the world as if he couldn't understand what all the fuss was about.

'I telephoned the boarding kennels yesterday after you had left, to see how he was,' Griff explained. 'They said the old devil was pining, so I brought him home last night.'

So he might not have been at home if she had walked across last night anyway.

The tense atmosphere at the neighbouring villa must be making a nervous wreck of her. What had she thought was under the bed—a snake? God, if only the ground would open up and swallow her!

But there was never a miracle around when you needed one, and somehow she was going to have to get through this second embarrassment of making a fool of herself in front of this man. It was becoming too much of a habit!

She put a hand up to her burning cheeks. 'I don't know what to say...'

Griff put the cat down—the ungrateful creature instantly going back under the bed—taking the sugar bowl from Sarah's unresisting fingers; she had forgotten she even held it! 'Your coffee will be getting cold again,' he realised with a sigh.

'Did you really throw two pots away before I arrived?' she asked breathlessly, following him back to the kitchen, grateful to him for not making too much of the fact that she had just made a complete idiot of herself again. A *snake*. God, how was she ever going to live down making such a mistake?

'I don't lie, Sarah.' Griff was suddenly serious. 'I never have the time for it. I'm rarely in one place long enough to bother with subterfuge,' he added in a harsh voice.

Maybe it was that very precariousness of his profession that had made Sandra Preston change her mind about committing herself to him after all. It could never be easy being married to a man you weren't sure was in danger or not.

But that didn't excuse the fact that the other woman had humiliated him in front of the whole world, making a much respected man a thing of ridicule and speculation.

'A glass of water would do me just as well,' she assured him as he poured away the cooling coffee and filled the mugs up again from the percolator.

'I'm determined you're going to taste the "Morgan coffee" before you leave today,' he said stubbornly. 'Let's go and sit by the pool and drink it,' he suggested as he picked up the two mugs. 'You can always finish watering the plants later. Unless you're in a hurry to leave again today?' He frowned at the thought, obviously not relishing the idea of being on his own again quite so soon, even if he had come here initially for solitude.

Clarissa would probably be hysterical when Sarah returned if she actually had to look after Stephen herself for too long, but for the moment Sarah just didn't care.

'Not for a little while, anyway,' she answered non-committally.

He looked so pleased she was sparing the time to have coffee with him that Sarah instantly felt guilty for not initially showing more enthusiasm for the idea herself.

But she was very conscious of the fact that he was a man who had been literally jilted at the altar, and the last thing she wanted was for him to think she would be interested in helping him salve his wounds in anything but a friendly capacity. She found him very attractive, and in other circumstances—for both of them!—would have welcomed the idea of getting to know him better. But at the moment he was far too vulnerable to actually know what he was doing. And the last thing Sarah needed right now was to be involved in a rebound love.

As a way of making amends for her tardiness she took a sip of the coffee he had been making such a fuss about her drinking.

The 'Morgan coffee' was so strong that Sarah almost choked on it, sure that if she left her spoon in it too long the metal would disintegrate!

She gave Griff an encouraging smile as he looked at her enquiringly, seeming unaffected by the strong brew himself.

He chuckled softly as her eyes actually watered when she took a second tentative sip. 'It's helped to keep me awake on more than one occasion,' he explained derisively.

Sarah blinked back the tears. 'With heartburn?' As soon as the words had left her lips she regretted having spoke them. This man's heart had to be more than 'burning' at the moment, and once again she had said the wrong thing. Couldn't she do anything right where this man was concerned? 'I'm so sorry——' she began.

'Don't be,' he cut in harshly. 'Just forget about all that, OK?'

She was trying to, and knew he was too, but it was very difficult to forget the circumstances of his being here at all. By rights he should probably have been off somewhere with Sandra, on their honeymoon.

'But, before we forget about it completely, I'd just like to thank you for not revealing my whereabouts to my avid colleagues the moment you realised who I was.' His derisive expression told her just what he thought of those 'colleagues' at this moment.

'It never occurred to me to do such a thing!' she gasped her indignation, her eyes wide.

'I had a feeling I could trust you.' He nodded. 'That's why I stayed put rather than disappearing again. You really are a nice lady, Sarah Williams.' Tawny-coloured eyes, narrowed with sensual appraisal, swept over the long length of her legs, the snug fit of her shorts, to the brief black camisole top she wore, before moving to the healthy shine of her confined hair and the fresh beauty of her face. 'A very nice lady,' he repeated softly.

And no man had ever made her feel so completely feminine with just a look before either, making her forget completely her indignation of a few minutes ago.

It would be sheer madness on her part to let herself become involved with this man; he was only looking for a little female reassurance after being jilted by the woman he loved, before disappearing back to his own world again.

Sheer madness, she warned herself again sternly.

Her hand trembled slightly as she smoothed back her hair self-consciously. 'I think I should be going now,' she began dismissively, doing her best to ignore the physical splendour of the man as he sat on the lounger so close to her own, their legs almost touching.

'Don't go yet, Sarah.' Griff put a hand lightly on her arm, his gaze troubled.

She drew in a shuddering breath. 'I really do have to go——'

He sighed. 'I meant what I said just now as a compliment, not the prelude to a pass,' he told her wearily. 'Besides, I thought you might stay and have a swim with me,' he added persuasively as he sensed her resolve was weakening.

This man was too clever by half, and the blue reflected water did look inviting, the sun shining hotly overhead.

This villa was the last on this rolling hillside, high trees about its perimeter affording them complete privacy from prying eyes.

It was very tempting to accept his invitation on a day when the temperature must be in the high eighties, and yet still she hesitated, unnerved by this man. 'I don't have a costume with me——'

'Borrow one of Virginia's,' he instantly offered as he saw victory looming. 'I noticed several of them in the changing-rooms. And, while the two of you might not have the same…measurements, I'm sure you could find something of hers that would do just for today,' he encouraged warmly.

While not exactly flat-chested, Sarah knew she certainly wasn't as voluptuous as his sister, a fact he seemed more than aware of too.

And why not? He was probably a connoisseur when it came to women, an expert in the way they looked if his beautiful fiancée was anything to go by!

Sarah accepted that she wasn't in the other woman's league when it came to looks or sophistication. But one thing she was sure of: she would never have put any man through the humiliation of being stood up at the altar!

She didn't like the way Sandra Preston had treated Griff, and if enjoying her company for a while helped take his mind off that then why shouldn't she do what he suggested?

It was with these rebellious thoughts in mind that Sarah went into one of the changing cubicles beside the pool.

As Griff had predicted, there were several bathing costumes in there, the two bikinis she picked up first completely unsuitable: the tops of them would have looked indecent, they were so big!

But at the bottom of the pile was a plain black costume that stretched over the body rather than fitted. It wasn't ideal by any means, but it was preferable to not being able to swim at all.

Griff was already in the water when she emerged out into the sunshine, his body sleek and powerful as he moved easily down the length of the pool.

Sarah climbed into the water before he turned and saw her, her movements easy and strong as she swam down the length of the pool to join him.

He turned to grin at her, rivulets of water cascading down his face from the wetness of his hair. 'You found something, then.' He looked at her admiringly.

Sarah ignored that appreciative look, treading water, completely out of her depth—and she had a feeling, if she wasn't careful, that it might not only be in the water. 'It's such a luxury to have a pool at your home like this.' She deliberately spoke of something less personal.

'Virginia married money,' Griff shrugged.

'Oh, I wasn't criticising,' Sarah rushed into speech, 'I just——'

'Will you stop apologising every time you open your mouth? I'm sure it isn't a usual characteristic,' Griff chided—although surely he knew that it was his having been jilted only days ago that was making her behave so tensely. 'It isn't necessary,' he assured her softly. 'And I said that Virginia married money; I didn't say that was the only reason she married Walter.'

She was behaving ridiculously, had to relax, or she was going to make even more of an idiot of herself. But Griff was right, she *was* usually so capable and sure of herself. 'I'm finding all this a little difficult,' she admitted ruefully.

He sobered. 'All what?'

'Well, what happened to you on Saturday——'

'I asked you to forget about that,' he sighed.

'I'm trying to,' she assured him. 'I—I just find it a little strange being here with you too, that's all. After all, you are a world-renowned reporter and——'

'I would never have thought you to be the star-struck type,' he teased.

'I'm not,' she scorned predictably. 'It's just that until yesterday you were just a name I read at the top of a newspaper article.'

'I'm just a man, like any other,' he dismissed easily.

He wasn't, and they both knew it, but she would at least find his company interesting; Ben had been the high-spot of the male company she had known the last ten days!

'Sarah?'

She looked up at him, smiling. 'I thought you invited me for a swim?'

He looked relieved that whatever the problem had been it seemed to have passed now. 'A length and back,' he challenged.

It was a strictly fun afternoon, Griff good company, as she had thought he would be.

He told her a little more about himself too, how he had travelled all over the world reporting since he was twenty years old. As he spoke of the last fifteen years he looked suddenly older, as if all that he had seen during that time was suddenly crowding in on him. But he hadn't gone into detail about any of those experiences, talking only of the countries he had found so interesting.

He took pity on her a little later and made her some lime juice rather than the 'Morgan coffee' that had caused her to shudder. His lime juice was definitely an improvement on that!

She loosened her hair about her shoulders so that it might dry in the sun, her hair already a lighter blonde after several days' bleaching in the hot sun, her skin tanned a golden brown, the bathing costume leaving her limbs and the gentle swell of the tops of her breasts bare.

'I'll have to be making a move to leave soon,' she finally said languidly, reluctant to move, if she was truthful, having found such peace and relaxation in Griff's company. After the maelstrom of the Forbes family it was like heaven on earth lying beside this pool!

Griff lay on the lounger at her side, his eyes closed as he rested, if not slept. His chest rose and fell in steady breathing, his face looking younger in repose, the lines relaxed from beside his nose and mouth, his lips slightly parted.

Almost as if he was waiting to be kissed ...

Sarah sat up with a start as a strange ringing sound came over the garden, only relaxing again slightly as she realised it was the doorbell. It was a strangely crude chiming bell for someone as elegant as Virginia Major.

'After complaining you haven't seen anyone for days you get two visitors in one day,' she teased him lightly.

Griff stretched lazily before sitting up. 'It's probably just the gardener again, wanting to be paid this time!' He laughed at the distaste on Sarah's face as the doorbell chimed again. 'Changing the doorbell was "one of the little jobs" Virginia told me I could do, while I was here, to make myself useful!' He stood up effortlessly. 'I think, now that I've heard how awful it is, I'll just leave it the way it is!'

Sarah couldn't help laughing at the wicked grin on his face. 'That isn't nice,' she chided lightly.

'Maybe I'll just disconnect it during my stay here,' he murmured thoughtfully as he crossed the lawn to the house.

Being an only child herself, Sarah had never had a brother to tease and taunt her. The latter might not have been very good, but it still might have been nice to have had a brother she could turn to. He might have been able to warn her away from Simon before she'd got so hurt!

'A friend of yours to see you, Sarah,' Griff called lightly across the garden.

She turned with a frown, her eyes widening with alarm as she saw Ben Forbes standing at Griff's side.

CHAPTER THREE

WHAT on earth was Ben doing *here*?

As his censorious gaze ran over the length of Sarah's body dressed only in the borrowed black bathing costume it became obvious what he believed *she* was doing here!

And maybe the situation did look damning to his eyes; she and Griff had obviously been lounging beside the pool together for some time, from the empty coffee-mugs and glasses on the ornate white table.

But they hadn't been doing anything wrong, and even if they had it would be none of Ben's business.

She had to be entitled to some time off from the family, surely?

She still couldn't get over Ben's being here at all. He had never been to the Major villa before, as far as she was aware. Certainly not while she had been here.

'I thought I would just come over and see what was keeping you,' he explained defiantly at her questioning look. 'You had been gone so long that I thought there must be something wrong,' he added accusingly.

Sarah's mouth tightened angrily at all the things he left unsaid but nevertheless implied. She had spent a lot of time with him the last ten days, hadn't had much choice in the circumstances, but to her he was just the eighteen-year-old son of her mother's friend. And yet he was trying to make her feel guilty about a completely innocent afternoon spent in the company of another man. It was too ridiculous to be taken seriously.

All Ben had actually achieved was making her feel angry at his arrogant behaviour. It smacked too much of his mother's selfishness!

'Well, as you can see,' she told him hardly, 'I'm perfectly all right and enjoying an afternoon in the sunshine.' And you and your mother can make of that what you will, Sarah added to herself silently; considering this was the only time she had had off since they'd arrived here, she knew she had to be entitled to it.

Tall and dark, although not as tall or dark as Griff, Ben looked slightly older than his years.

Although his actions this afternoon showed he certainly wasn't more mature in his behaviour!

She hadn't seen much of Ben over the years; first of all he had been away from the family at boarding-school, and then at college, but she had been pleasantly surprised by how nice he could be this last week or so.

But what she didn't accept, couldn't accept, was that he had actually dared to come here, checking up on her. Because she certainly didn't believe the excuse he had used about thinking something might have happened to her.

'As I can see,' he repeated coldly before shooting a knowing look in Griff's direction. 'I thought you were supposed to be over here working.' He met Sarah's furious gaze challengingly.

Her breath caught in her throat. Just exactly what did he mean by *that* remark? This whole incident was turning into one of the most embarrassing moments of her life.

'I've finished watering the plants,' she answered abruptly. 'If you come with me, Ben, I'll just show you to the door,' she added firmly, crossing the lawn to his side, wishing she had a robe she could pull on as he continued to look at her assessingly, not particularly wanting to scramble into her shorts and top as if she had something to hide.

Griff shot her a frowning look as she passed him to grasp Ben's arm firmly as she forced him to turn and walk back through the villa to the front door.

'I'll see you back at our villa,' she told him through gritted teeth.

'What are you doing with him?' Ben demanded, for the moment seeming unaware of the imminent danger of Sarah's temper if she should completely lose it.

'I'll see you later, Ben,' she repeated in a voice so meticulously steady that it should have been an indication of her fury.

One that Ben still didn't pick up on! 'Mother isn't at all happy about your disappearing act— Sarah!' he yelped as she opened the door and pushed him outside before he could even think of stopping her, the door as quickly closed in his face.

Sarah stood just inside the villa, breathing deeply, too angry to even move just yet. How dared he do that to her? His damned family seemed to have the impression she should be grateful they had brought her to the south of France with them at all!

She couldn't think what had made Ben behave in that way. Until a few minutes ago she had thought him the nicest of the Forbes family; now she wasn't so sure...

Facing Griff again after that embarrassing scene wasn't going to be easy. She hated to think what conclusions he must have made from Ben's behaviour...!

Griff wasn't beside the pool when she got outside again, and so she quickly took advantage of his absence to go inside the changing-room and get back into her own clothes.

Ben's visit aside—if only that were possible!—she really would have to be leaving soon.

Griff would probably be glad to see the back of her now—he certainly wasn't in the mood for unexpected visitors, supposed friends of hers, invading his privacy. Damn Ben!

One thing she knew for certain: she would make very sure when she saw him later that he knew she wouldn't allow him to repeat his behaviour.

Slight noises coming from the kitchen alerted her to Griff's whereabouts, and she entered the room a little apprehensively.

Griff turned to smile at her, having pulled on denims and a loose T-shirt himself since leaving the poolside. His head tilted quizzically to one side as he saw her anxious expression. 'Whatever you do, don't apologise,' he said ruefully.

'But——'

'No buts,' he teased lightly. 'I suppose I should have realised there was bound to be a boyfriend somewhere——'

'Ben isn't my boyfriend!' Sarah cut in protestingly. 'He's——' she broke off abruptly, realising what she was doing. It was surely of no interest to Griff Morgan whether Ben was her boyfriend or not! Although she would rather he knew the facts as they were rather than the erroneous impression Ben's behaviour just now must have given him. 'He's Clarissa's son,' she stated firmly. 'The friend of my mother that I'm here to help out.'

'Not the nine-year-old, definitely,' Griff mocked.

'No,' she conceded tightly. 'But he's definitely a *boy* too!'

Griff's mouth quirked. 'A little over-anxious, maybe,' he acknowledged. 'But then, he has a serious case of being attracted to you.'

Sarah's cheeks were flushed at the idea. 'Don't be ridiculous!'

Griff gave her a searching look before shrugging dismissively, as if the subject was of little interest to him anyway. 'How about helping me get a meal ready?' he suggested lightly. 'There's salad, and——'

'I can't stay, I'm afraid,' she said regretfully, wishing she could stay and share the salad and French bread he had out on the work-top, having come to love the bread especially since coming here. 'I have to go back and get the family meal,' she grimaced.

'Oh, well. Another time,' Griff accepted easily.

Too easily as far as Sarah was concerned. He might have at least acted slightly disappointed by her refusal, even if he wasn't really!

'Do you want me to come in tomorrow?' she frowned. 'Or do you think you can manage now while your sister is away?'

He shrugged. 'I probably could manage—although I can't guarantee that the plants would survive! But I'm also not sure yet how long I shall be staying, so maybe you had better continue to come in as you have been.'

Very informative. He certainly wasn't giving anything of his plans away. 'That's all right, then,' she said flatly, wishing the afternoon hadn't taken such a down-turn. 'Perhaps I'll see you tomorrow,' she added lightly.

'Perhaps.' He nodded vaguely, continuing to prepare the salad.

'Bye,' she prompted frustratedly. They had been getting along so well together until that untimely interruption. 'I'll see myself out, shall I?'

'Sorry.' He straightened, smiling lightly. 'I'm forgetting my manners.' He walked out to the door with her. 'Virginia would be horrified,' he added mockingly.

'I'm hardly a guest,' Sarah said drily.

'I've enjoyed your company,' he told her warmly. 'I only hope I haven't caused too much trouble between yourself and Ben.'

'I told you—— Oh, never mind,' she dismissed irritably; if he didn't want to believe there was nothing between herself and Ben then nothing she said was going to convince him otherwise. Unless she told him she was here recovering from a disastrous love-affair herself, and she had no intention of doing that! 'Thanks for the swim.' She nodded abruptly.

'Any time,' he smiled, standing in the doorway, watching her as she walked over to her car.

Sarah wanted to say something, anything, so that the afternoon shouldn't end in this flat way. But there was nothing she could say that wouldn't look as if she was romantically interested in *him*.

And, attractive as he was, she really couldn't allow herself to be attracted to him.

Griff was only here at all to get over the fickleness of a woman—he wouldn't be interested in becoming involved with another one. And even if he was it would only be in a temporary way, a fleeting affair to rid himself of the memory of the beautiful Sandra. Sarah was no longer willing to be second best to another woman, had learnt her lesson the hard way.

And wasn't she actually appreciating Griff's company more than she usually might because of the tension and unhappiness she was experiencing at the Forbes villa?

Oh, she had no doubt she would have found Griff Morgan fascinating at any time, but in the circumstances he was becoming like a lifeline she was starting to cling to while the madness at the Forbes villa seemed to get worse and worse.

It was a situation she would have to be wary of.

She gave Griff a brief wave of her hand as she drove out of the driveway, determined not even to glance in her mirror today.

Her tension rose even as she approached the pink and white villa, knowing by the air of quiet slumber outside that the family must have already deserted the poolside and be inside somewhere.

Sarah didn't doubt that inside the villa would be far from quietly slumbering!

Clothes that had been brought up from the poolside lay scattered all over the lounge, the tray of glasses at least having been brought up too but put down haphazardly on the coffee-table, one of them having fallen over, its red contents—whatever they were!—staining the plastic tray.

Sally and Stephen were seated at the dining-room table, squabbling over whose turn it was to go at chess. Stephen ended that particular argument by tipping the board over and scattering the pieces everywhere. Sally let out a wail to arouse the whole household, and indeed Clarissa, at least, appeared from the kitchen, wielding a sharp-looking knife in one hand and a tomato in the other—Sarah could only hope

she intended to use the knife to slice the tomato!—her face flushed with harassment.

'What on earth is all the noise about in here,
Sarah!' She pounced furiously as she spotted
her across the room, blue eyes narrowed accusingly. 'Where the hell have you been all afternoon?' she demanded resentfully.

It had been obvious to Sarah after spending
only a couple of days in the constant company
of Clarissa Forbes that her gentle mother didn't
really know her old school-friend very well at
all, that the other woman's language left a lot to
be desired, and that she could be an out and out
cat when thwarted. She was the complete op-
posite of Sarah's mother. And yet the friendship had flourished all these years. It was
anyone's guess why!

But there was no way Sarah was going to tell
Clarissa about Griff Morgan's presence in the
neighbouring villa if she didn't have to; the poor
man wouldn't have a minute's peace if Clarissa
found out they had such a well-known neighbour.

She shrugged now, not at all perturbed by the
other woman's aggression. 'Didn't Ben tell
you?'

'Ben?' Clarissa echoed sharply. 'Why the hell should——? Stephen, will you stop that whining?' She finally lost her temper with the 'crocodile tears' that had begun to fall as soon as his mother had come through from the kitchen, Stephen being determined he wasn't going to be the one caught in the wrong, and if he got in first he wasn't likely to be!

'But, Mummy, he——'

'Don't you start, Sally,' her mother snapped irritably. 'Well, at least you've turned up now.' She turned back coldly to Sarah, crossing the room to thrust the knife and tomato into her hands. 'I have one of my headaches.' It was said accusingly. 'I need to lie down if Roger and I are to go out to dinner this evening. The children need their tea,' she added dismissively before flouncing unconcernedly from the room on her way to her bedroom, the chaos she had left behind her completely forgotten now that she had found someone to shift the responsibility on to.

Within minutes Sarah had Stephen and Sally organised laying the table—much against their will, and still bickering and fighting, but they *were* doing it!—and she had the steaks cooking beneath the grill as she tossed the salad in a bowl.

'So you're back, are you?'

She took her time turning to face Ben, deliberately so, knowing that if she didn't she was really going to lose her temper with this particular young man.

He looked hot and sweaty, as if he had been for a long walk since he'd left her. And perhaps he had, but Sarah had far from forgiven him for causing her such embarrassment earlier.

'Yes, I'm back,' she answered him calmly. 'But if you ever talk to me like that again, in or out of company, you will know the full force of my anger.' Her words were all the more effective because of the quietness of her voice. 'Now do I——?'

'Who was that man?' Ben demanded, his face flushed with indignation.

'——make myself clear?' she completed firmly, totally ignoring his question.

He met her gaze defiantly for several long, tension-filled minutes.

Sarah had never before seen such a likeness to Clarissa in this eldest Forbes child. Of the three she had so far found Ben the most amenable; but not when things didn't go his way, apparently.

With one last furious glare in her direction he turned on his heel and left the room.

Somehow Sarah didn't think he would be joining them for the evening meal!

She took several deep breaths to calm her own jangling nerves. Another two weeks of this and she was going to need a holiday to get over this one. That, or a strait-jacket!

'Where *did* you go this afternoon?'

Sarah turned to find Sally hovering at her elbow, her youthfully beautiful face alight with curiosity.

This young woman, tall and leggy like her mother, but with her father's dark colouring, had been named after Sarah as a compliment to Clarissa's old school-friend. So that no confusion should ensue the younger Sarah had duly been designated the name Sally in its stead.

Anyone less like herself Sarah thought it would be difficult to find. Or perhaps she was being unfair; Sally was at that awkward age, not yet considered quite a woman, but definitely not still a child either, and it was difficult for people to know quite how to treat her. Consequently they tended to waver between the two, and usually failed dismally to communicate with

Sally on any level. Sarah knew she was as guilty of this as the family.

The two of them certainly weren't the best of friends, and Sarah viewed her friendliness now with suspicion, shrugging dismissively. 'It took a little longer at the villa than I had expected.' She went over to check the steaks under the grill.

Sally leant in the doorway. 'I thought Ben mentioned a man . . .'

'Then you had better talk to Ben about it, hadn't you?' Sarah said uninterestedly, knowing that Sally wouldn't do that; the eldest of the Forbes children weren't yet of an age where they could appreciate each other's worth.

Sally remained in the doorway, her frustration with the conversation tangible. Finally she flounced off, and seconds later there was the predictable sound of a door banging, followed by over-loud pop music being played.

Another enjoyable evening with the Forbes family!

It only needed Stephen to start on her and they would have a hat-trick!

But the next outburst came from Clarissa. Apparently Roger had decided he didn't really feel like going out this evening after all, and Clarissa was absolutely furious about it.

'If that's the way you feel,' she stormed into the lounge ahead of a surprisingly stubbornly determined husband, 'I'll just have to get Ben to take me out instead!'

'Clarissa——'

'He's old enough, Roger,' she told him defiantly, her cheeks hot with anger, the red body-hugging dress she wore provocative to say the least, her long legs tanned and bare beneath its short length.

It was amazing how Clarissa changed the rules to suit what she wanted to do; she *wanted* to go out for the evening, and so Ben was no longer a 'child' to be left at home but completely mature enough to accompany her.

It was no wonder the children were a rebellious mass of contradictions.

Of course, there was no argument from Ben about this suggestion, and he did look very handsome in a suit borrowed from his father, not having brought anything that formal with him; he obviously knew from experience what his evenings were going to be like when they went on holiday!

He shot Sarah a disdainful glance before accompanying his mother out of the door.

Oh, dear, her only ally in this household had now deserted her!

'Cheer up, Sarah,' Roger drawled, having eaten the salad and steaks his children had refused. 'Just think of the peaceful evening we're going to have!'

She returned his smile ruefully, knowing that for most of the time he was slightly in awe of the fact that someone as beautifully vivacious as Clarissa could be his wife. But he obviously needed a break from all that on occasion!

'A game of chess?' he suggested lightly.

The highlight of all her evenings spent here! But at least Roger was a worthy opponent.

As evenings went on this holiday, it stood out as one of the better ones.

'How cosy,' Sally drawled. 'I'm sure this isn't what Mummy thought you had in mind when you said you wanted "a quiet evening"!'

Sarah looked up sharply from the board where she and Roger were just playing the deciding game out of three. Neither of them was an expert, but they were at least well-matched.

Sally's suggestive tone as she viewed them mockingly, from across the room, spoilt all that.

'So you've decided to come out of your bedroom at last, have you?' Roger seemed to have decided to ignore his daughter's insulting tone. 'There's food in the fridge, if you're hungry.'

'I'm not,' she scorned in a voice that made Sarah itch to slap her. But Roger was her parent—it was up to him to reprimand her if he felt she needed it. He didn't. 'I'll leave the two of you alone again, as you seem to be having such a good time together,' she added tauntingly.

'Leave her,' Roger advised wearily as Sarah would have risen angrily and followed the young girl as she left the room. 'I've been assured she will outgrow these moods.' He shook his head disbelievingly.

She had better; Sarah was fast coming to the end of her patience where this family was concerned. Mother or no mother, she would leave them to it the moment she just couldn't take any more.

But she would be leaving Griff Morgan behind too if she did that, a little voice inside her warned.

She gave a start of surprise at this unbidden thought.

What did it matter if she never saw Griff Morgan again? He was nothing to her.

Was he . . . ?

CHAPTER FOUR

'COME and join us.'

'Us' consisted of Sally, a languid Jasper stretched on her bare legs as she sat in a poolside chair at the Majors villa, wearing only a brief bikini, and Griff Morgan, sitting in an accompanying chair, wearing only a pair of bathing trunks, light blue this time, making his tan look even darker!

Sarah had had no idea when Sally had disappeared earlier this morning that she had come over to the villa, had assumed she had gone off on one of the sulky walks she had been indulging in since they'd arrived here.

But from the look of her, and from the confidence of her invitation to Sarah, Sally had been here for some time, and had made herself very much at home!

As for the damned cat, after the way he had behaved with her yesterday, when he had half scared her to death, draping himself all over Sally was absolutely disgraceful!

Griff seemed to be following her line of thought with amusement, his own reaction to this unexpected guest not apparent as yet, although on the surface he didn't appear too perturbed.

Or perhaps he just didn't realise yet that his privacy had been well and truly intruded upon, that Clarissa was sure to learn of his presence here now, and Clarissa was even more determined than her daughter, wouldn't give him a moment's privacy.

But that was Griff's problem, Sarah told herself firmly; she wasn't some sort of watch-dog service for him.

He must have known he was taking the risk of being recognised wherever he disappeared to. It would be up to him to convince Clarissa she didn't want to reveal his whereabouts to the Press. He probably had charm enough...

Sour grapes?

No, of course not, she defended; she was just a little disconcerted to find Sally here, that was all.

'Not just now,' she called down to them from the villa steps. 'I'm just going to see to the plants——'

'I told you I would do that today,' Sally cut in lightly, her gaze challenging.

The little madam had even lied to get herself admitted to the villa!

But Griff hadn't *had* to invite her to stay after she'd completed the task . . .

'So you did,' she accepted tightly. 'Well, in that case, I'll leave you two to it,' whatever 'it' was!

'Do come and join us,' Griff repeated the invitation, standing up in one fluid movement, crossing the paved area beside the pool before padding across the grass to stand in front of Sarah. 'Please,' he added desperately, for her ears alone.

Sarah's anger at Sally's duplicity disappeared as quickly as it had arisen as she sensed his urgent request for help, her mouth quirking with amusement as she glanced across to where Sally still posed in the chair. 'Having a few problems?' she taunted softly as she turned back to Griff.

He looked even more harassed. 'That particular young lady is a bundle of mischief marked "trouble"!'

Didn't she know it! Sally was one of the prime people making her stay here so unbearable; she should have guessed the young girl would try something like this. 'And the two of you seem to be having such fun together,' Sarah mocked.

'Sarah!' he said warningly.

She grinned up at him, the first time she had had anything to smile about since she'd seen him yesterday. 'Well, if you really would like me to stay for a while...?'

'I insist upon it.' He frowned. 'I'd get down on my knees and beg, but I think Sally might become a little suspicious if I did that!'

'When you put it like that...' Sarah shrugged.

'Yes?'

'Have you tried plying her with the "Morgan coffee"?' she delayed.

He raised his eyes heavenwards. 'She liked it!'

Sarah's mouth twitched at his obvious disgust. 'Then it's obviously more serious than I thought.'

'Very funny.' Griff grimaced at her humour in the face of his predicament.

Sarah nodded. 'Sally seems to have a "serious case of being attracted to you",' she repeated his words of yesterday concerning herself and Ben in an effort to show him how these infatuations could happen without the slightest encouragement. After Ben's behaviour to her the evening before she was inclined to think Griff could be right about that particular observation. And Sally was at a stage in her young life where she was attracted to any male who was reasonably good-looking and mature enough to offer her something more interesting than boys her own age.

'Maybe we should gang up on the spoilt little brats and show them we aren't interested in either of them,' Griff muttered.

'What are the two of you talking about over there?' Sally had sat forward and was watching them with narrowed eyes.

'And to think I was complaining about my lack of company yesterday,' Griff sighed longingly.

Sarah laughed softly. 'We had better go and join her.'

'You mean you will stay for a while?' he pounced eagerly.

She nodded. 'But I think I should warn you, Sally can be very determined,' she told him softly over her shoulder as she strolled across the grass to join Sally by the pool.

The cat had jumped down from Sally's legs now, purring softly as he padded over to Sarah, twining himself in and out of her legs.

'Creep,' Sarah told him good-naturedly as she bent down to absently stroke one furry ear.

Sally was looking at her speculatively. 'No wonder you wanted to keep *him* to yourself!'

Sarah turned sharply to look at Griff behind her, but he seemed to have disappeared inside the villa, probably to get fresh drinks for them all, she realised. 'You do know who he is, Sally?' She frowned at the young girl.

'Of course I do,' she dismissed. 'And how he was left standing at the altar on Saturday. Sandra Preston must be a pretty stupid woman,' she scorned, 'letting someone like him escape.'

'Sally,' she began impatiently, 'we can't know the full circumstances——'

'*I* wouldn't care what the "circumstances" were if I could be with a man like Griff Morgan,' Sally told her eagerly.

That was the difference between Sally's naïveté and Sarah's having learnt the hard way that it wasn't always as simple as that. The difference between still being a child and growing up...

'His fiancée obviously had her reasons for what she did.' Sarah shrugged dismissively.

'Stupidity,' Sally nodded knowingly. 'And she's his *ex*-fiancée,' she muttered, directing a dazzling smile over Sarah's shoulder.

It didn't need two guesses to realise Griff had rejoined them, and he had brought out with him a jug of fresh lemonade and three glasses.

Looking at him, so tall and powerfully muscular, Sarah had to admit she couldn't help agreeing with Sally at that moment. It could possibly be the first time—and was probably the last!—that she had agreed with the young girl, but she couldn't help thinking Sandra Preston had to be stupid, too!

It was embarrassing to watch Sally's immature flirting with Griff over the next hour, although Griff, despite the impression he had given earlier, seemed to be handling it very capably, treating Sally with the casualness of an older brother or uncle.

And Sally didn't like that at all!

'You must come over for dinner one evening,' she suggested suddenly, sitting up.

Sarah frowned as Griff couldn't hide his expression of dismay; socialising was the last thing he felt like doing. 'Sally, I don't think——'

'Tonight?' Sally continued excitedly, completely ignoring Sarah.

Griff drew in a deep breath, obviously thinking fast. 'I'm sure your parents——'

But not fast enough!

'Mummy adores dinner guests,' Sally determinedly cut in on his objections, with more enthusiasm than actual truth; Clarissa did enjoy having guests for dinner, as long as she didn't have to actually do any of the work involved in catering for them. Which she usually didn't. 'And you would be a lovely diversion for Mummy and Daddy,' Sally continued. 'They seem a little . . . bored by each other's company at the moment.' She shot a sideways glance at Sarah after this last remark.

Her eyes widened. Just what did Sally mean by that? Really, she shouldn't have let herself be persuaded from giving this young girl a verbal dressing down the evening before!

Griff was watching the optical exchange between them with curiosity, finally shrugging his shoulders as neither of them seemed about to add anything to the conversation. 'I really don't think I would be good company for them at the moment——'

'Nonsense,' Sally dismissed. 'I'm sure you're good company at any time,' she added coyly.

His fiancée obviously hadn't thought so, Sarah thought drily, and she could see Griff found the effusive compliment embarrassing.

His mouth tightened with irritation. 'I'm actually working while I'm here,' he told Sally firmly.

'Working?' Blue eyes widened. 'But I thought you were here because——'

'I'm working,' Griff repeated determinedly, 'actually.' He stood up in one fluid movement, and Sarah couldn't stop herself watching the play of muscles across his body.

He was so obviously masculine, exuded a sensual magnetism Sarah was fast finding fascinating, her breath shallow in her chest.

If only Griff weren't here recovering from a broken heart...

If only *she* weren't here recovering from a broken heart...

'I should be working now,' he continued briskly, his narrow-eyed gaze studiously avoiding Sarah's, needing her support very badly just now.

She took the hint, even if Sally didn't, straightening in her chair. 'I think it's time we were leaving now, Sally.'

'But——'

'Griff is a busy man,' she added firmly, standing up, her legs long and golden beneath the brief purple shorts she wore with a yellow and purple T-shirt.

As she had pulled on the garish clothing this morning, hastily bought for this time away in the sunshine, Sarah had known she would never be seen wearing them in England!

'And I thought you were supposed to be going shopping to Juan-les-Pins today with your mother,' she reminded pointedly, knowing that Clarissa's anger, and the lure of the boutiques in the popular resort, would be too much for the young girl.

'Oh, God, yes!' Sally shot up, grabbing up her pile of clothes from the grass. 'I'd better go,' she told Griff apologetically, not sparing Sarah a second glance as she hurried away.

Griff watched her go, looking like a man who felt as if he had just been run over by a steam-roller!

Sarah looked up at him with amusement; she knew how he felt—she had been feeling the same way herself for the past twelve days!

'Is the mother anything like that?' Griff finally asked weakly.

Her mouth quirked as she restrained her humour. 'Worse!' she said with feeling.

'Oh, God...!' He sat down again heavily, running a hand over his brow.

Sarah held back her humour now with effort, green eyes glowing with suppressed amusement.

Griff looked across at her with an air of desperation. 'How am I going to get through this dinner invitation?'

Because both of them knew the invitation would be forthcoming!

'Clarissa and Roger can be good company,' she told him slowly, knowing Clarissa was sure to be at her most dazzlingly charming with such a distinguished guest.

Griff eyed her sourly. 'You don't sound too sure about that.'

She grinned. 'Well, it promises to be an interesting evening anyway.'

'With me as the "interest",' he realised with a grimace. 'I suppose it was too much to hope I was going to be able to come here and achieve the anonymity that I wanted,' he sighed.

'I hope you don't think that I——'

'I've told you what I think of you, Sarah Williams, and nothing has happened since then to change my opinion,' he cut in lightly. 'You're a nice woman. And no, I don't think you went blabbing my presence here all over the valley.'

'What happened was that Sally overheard Ben talking to me about you——'

'Still giving you a hard time, is he?' Griff nodded understandingly.

She hadn't seen that particular young man yet this morning, and had understood from a bleary-eyed Clarissa as she'd groped her way to the coffee-pot earlier that they hadn't got in until three o'clock this morning.

'I'll survive,' Sarah shrugged dismissively. 'And now, if you want to work, I had better be going.' She stood up.

'Er...?'

She looked down at Griff, her heart skipping its usual beat as she did so. 'Yes?'

'Sally never did get around to watering the plants,' he told her with a grimace.

Sarah looked at him with disbelief for several seconds, and then she burst out laughing.

'I might have guessed!' She shook her head. 'I'll go and do them now.'

'And I'll go and get us some lunch—yes?' he prompted hopefully.

Sarah frowned down at him. 'But I thought you had some work to do?'

'I do.' Griff nodded with a grin. 'Lunch is top of the list.'

She shook her head regretfully. 'If Clarissa and Sally are going out I'll have to get back. Three helpless males left alone together is disastrous!' she added drily.

'They obviously weren't brought up properly,' he dismissed.

'Obviously not,' she acknowledged. 'I really will have to move,' she said quickly after a glance at her watch; she couldn't spend all day here bandying teasing remarks with Griff, enjoyable as it might be.

For all that Griff had made light of the suggestion that he really was here working, there were sheets of writing paper and notebooks all over the dining table. Sarah didn't presume to look at them, going straight into the kitchen to fill up the watering-can.

Watering plants and flowers was one of the mundane jobs she had done as a junior nurse.

As a senior staff nurse, with promotion to sister in sight, she had thought these days were over.

It was a step in the right direction that she was beginning to think about the promotion she had so recently lost simply because she had made the mistake of loving the wrong man.

Simon . . .

She had tried so hard the last few days not to even think of him, when really she knew she would have to sort out her feelings for him at some time. How strange she should think of him now, when she was with another man she found so attractive.

She went out to the courtyard, still deep in thought, climbing the small stepladder to reach the hanging baskets of deeply scented flowers.

Simon, with the silky blond hair and too-handsome face.

A consultant at the hospital where Sarah also worked, he had bowled Sarah over from the start. The miracle of it was, or so it had seemed to Sarah at the time, that he'd found her just as attractive.

Simon had asked her out once, twice, casually at first, and then more seriously. Or, at least, it had seemed more seriously to Sarah . . .

But Simon had told her, eventually, without the slightest hint of hesitation, that marriage between them was out of the question. Marriage had never been an essential to her, but some sort of commitment to their relationship had.

Sarah had known, hard as it was to accept, that she was wasting her life loving a man like Simon.

Breaking away from him hadn't been easy, especially as he'd been far from ready for their relationship to end, but——

'I think you could be over-watering that one,' Griff remarked drily from below her.

Sarah suddenly realised the hanging basket she was watering had water pouring as quickly out of the bottom of it, where it had soaked up as much as it was able!

'You were miles away.' Griff smiled up at her, half questioning.

She wasn't about to confide to anyone what an abject fool she had been. 'This sort of weather,' she looked up pointedly at the clear blue sky and hot, penetrating sun, 'makes you feel sleepy. I—— Oh!'

Looking up was probably her mistake. Whatever the reason, she momentarily lost her balance, clutching at thin air when she tried to steady herself, toppling over completely, the watering-can flying out of her hand across the courtyard.

It all seemed to happen in slow motion. One minute she was standing on top of the steps, the next she was falling through the warm air on her way to the tiled courtyard.

Strong arms caught and held her before she could make that painful landing, and her heart skipped a beat of relief at Griff's timely intervention, her arms clinging instinctively about his neck.

And then her heart skipped another beat—for a completely different reason!

Griff's flesh felt warm and electrifying beneath her touch, muscles rippling against her softness, her breath suddenly catching in her throat as she looked up and their gazes clashed.

Griff's eyes deepened in colour to gold, a nerve pulsing in his cheek, an expression on his face unlike any Sarah had ever seen there before. He was neither cynical nor amused, but completely serious, and yet not harshly so. He just looked——

Sarah didn't have any more time to decide how he looked, gasping slightly as his lips came down gently on hers, softly exploring, Sarah instantly responding to the warm caress.

Griff finally raised his head, their breaths mingling as their faces were only inches apart still.

'I think——' She broke off in embarrassment at how shaky and gruff her voice sounded, swallowing hard. 'I think perhaps you should put me down now.' She looked pointedly to where Griff still held her tightly in his arms.

He broke her gaze with effort. 'Yes. Of course.' He lowered her slowly to the ground, but he didn't release her. 'Sarah...?'

What was the point in questioning it...what was the point in questioning any of it—when she still wanted so much for him to kiss her again?

And when he did she melted against him, responding instinctively.

Passion flared, flamed, consumed, would have completely engulfed if they hadn't been interrupted.

Sarah caressed the heat of Griff's back and shoulders, feeling the force of his passion against her as they strained towards each other for a closer contact they knew they could attain, if only——

The huge bee that buzzed too close to them to be ignored put an end to 'if only', Sarah moving away from Griff with a startled cry; she had never seen bees as big as the ones here in France, huge black things, almost like hornets, and so attracted to the honeysuckle that grew up one wall of the courtyard.

It flew off to the honeysuckle now, leaving Sarah and Griff simply staring at each other, Sarah pale as she realised the enormity of what had just happened between them.

Griff met her gaze warmly. 'I've wanted to kiss you since the moment I first saw you.'

She swallowed hard, knowing she had been wanting it too, still quivering from the reality of it. 'I—Sandra...?' she reminded weakly.

He closed his eyes, breathing deeply, his hands clenched at his sides. 'Sarah, I—— Things aren't—always what they seem.' He looked at her regretfully.

All she knew was that until five days ago Griff had been going to marry another woman, would be married to her now if Sandra Preston hadn't decided not to turn up for the wedding.

Sarah turned away abruptly. 'I have to go——'

'Sarah!' He grasped her arm, turning her to face him. 'Sarah, I——'

'I really do have to go,' she insisted brusquely. 'They will be wondering where I've got to.' She broke away.

'Sarah!' Griff called after her pleadingly.

'I—have—to—go!' She ran from the villa, too frightened to look back this time, crunching the car into gear before driving away, tears streaming down her cheeks.

She had loved Simon, and yet she had *never* responded in that wanton way with him.

Had loved Simon?

Oh, dear God, what was *happening* to her?

CHAPTER FIVE

'How could you try and keep that absolutely delicious man to yourself?'

Sarah looked up at Clarissa from the pool, where she was playing a game of catch with Stephen.

She didn't need to ask who the 'absolutely delicious man' was; Sally had obviously told her mother about Griff while they were out.

'I didn't try to keep him to myself, Clarissa,' she answered calmly, her panic of this morning under control now, if not forgotten. 'I simply respected the man's privacy.'

Clarissa looked buoyant from her afternoon's shopping—and from the prospect of having a handsome single man in the neighbouring villa, Sarah didn't doubt.

'What he needs is company, not to shut himself away like that,' Clarissa stated determinedly. 'I'm going to telephone him right now and invite him over for dinner.'

And no doubt Griff would be 'persuaded' into accepting, no matter what his true feelings about the invitation might be.

Sarah knew, better than anyone, how persuasively charming the other woman could be when she set out to be—she was here in France with the family, wasn't she, when from the outset it had been the last thing she'd wanted to do?

Clarissa smiled in anticipation. 'Yes, I think it would be rather——'

'Mummy,' Stephen protested impatiently, 'we were playing!'

'Sorry, darling.' She gave him one of her dazzling smiles that said her thoughts were really elsewhere. 'Do we have anything nice in for dinner, Sarah?'

As if it really had anything to do with her! 'I was going to cook kebabs,' she muttered.

'That will do fine.' The other woman nodded distractedly. 'I'll throw together one of my fruit salads for dessert. I'm sure Griff Morgan will appreciate a home-cooked meal,' she added with satisfaction. 'I'll just go and telephone him.' She wandered off, already plotting and planning in her head, if her expression was anything to go by.

'And we can get back to our game.' Stephen glared after his mother.

Sarah carried on playing with him in a half-hearted way, glancing at the villa from time to time, intensely curious as to what had been the outcome of Clarissa's telephone call to Griff. She didn't doubt, for all Clarissa's powers of persuasion, that if Griff really didn't want to come here for dinner then he wouldn't. After this morning, she wondered if he would want to see *her* again so soon.

She didn't even want to think how she felt about the idea of seeing *him* again!

One glance at the formally laid dining table when she came up from the pool a little later and she knew Griff was going to be arriving here very soon.

But laying the table in the way that she wanted it, and 'throwing together one of her fruit salads' was the only contribution Clarissa made towards dinner, disappearing an hour before she said Griff was due to arrive so that she could shower and get ready for their guest.

Preparing kebabs for seven people, putting all that meat and assorted vegetables on to skewers, wasn't as easy as it should have been, and was time-consuming, to say the least.

'Like some help?'

She looked over at Ben warily as he stood in the doorway. She hadn't seen him since their exchange the night before, had no reason to suppose he felt any more friendly towards her than he had then.

Ben saw that look, grimacing slightly. 'I realise I behaved like an idiot yesterday. Could we just forget it?'

Sarah straightened. 'You do realise who is coming to dinner this evening?' She arched mocking brows.

'I realise,' he nodded. 'And I also know exactly who our neighbour is now, the disappointment he had on Saturday, and how badly I misjudged the situation between the two of you yesterday.'

He might not have felt so confident of that if he had walked in on Griff and herself today!

'As long as you do realise that.' She remained cool. 'I would appreciate some help.'

They worked together in companionable silence, Sarah at last having ten minutes, once everything was prepared, to go and get changed herself.

She would rather not have had to be present at this dinner at all this evening, but it would only draw attention to that fact if she attempted to get out of it.

Besides, part of her did very much want to see Griff again. The part of her that had also enjoyed his kisses . . .

Roger was choosing the wine when she got back to the kitchen, looking across at her with a rueful smile. 'Only the best tonight for our distinguished guest.' He made a face, taking the cork out of a bottle of red wine to let it breathe, as Sarah's father had used to say.

Strange; she hadn't indulged in thoughts of her father for some time now, occasionally taking out little memories of him to be enjoyed when she was alone. She missed him very much, had first wanted to become a nurse because she wanted to help prevent other people's fathers dying so young the way that hers had. She wasn't sure that she did that, but she did at least try.

She made a show of checking on the food. 'Has Mr Morgan arrived yet?' she asked as casually as she could. 'I'll need to know so that I can start cooking the kebabs,' she attempted to explain her interest.

Roger didn't look surprised. 'Clarissa has taken him down to the pool.' He grimaced. 'As if he hasn't seen a pool before, even a kidney-shaped one like ours!'

Sarah was glad of the breathing-space now that she actually knew Griff was here, whatever Clarissa's motives might be.

But the awkward moment couldn't be put off forever, and all too soon she served the kebabs and accompanying rice and Ben went off in search of everyone so that they could sit down and eat.

For all that she hadn't had much time to spend on her appearance earlier, Sarah had chosen her dress with care, in the knowledge of Clarissa's beautiful clothes, wearing a simple black dress that finished just above her knee, her legs bare and tanned, the heels on her shoes of medium height, enough to make her appear taller but not so high that she couldn't walk in them, her make-up kept to a minimum with the tan she had acquired, her lip-gloss pale pink, her hair plaited neatly down her spine from the top of her crown. Her image in the bedroom mirror before she'd left her room had shown that she looked cool and composed.

She only wished she felt that way too!

Griff, when he at last strolled into the lounge, was dressed more formally than she had previously seen him, wearing a cream shirt but no tie, the shirt unbuttoned at his throat, beige trousers fitting him loosely, as was fashionable, his hands thrust into his trouser pockets. His hair was brushed back from his face, his expression deliberately bland, although his gaze sharpened as he saw Sarah across the room.

She looked away quickly. 'Dinner is ready in the other room,' she announced to the room in general.

The whole family was there, even Stephen allowed to stay up and meet their distinguished guest, although he was to go to bed straight after dessert.

Clarissa and Sally sat either side of Griff at the oval table, Sarah sandwiched between Ben and Stephen, knowing, even though it was Clarissa's treat that he should stay up and join them, that she was expected to supervise Stephen during the meal. Not that Sarah particularly minded being relegated to the role of nanny for the evening; it meant she didn't have to join in the conversation.

It was bad enough that Clarissa and Sally were vying for Griff's attention!

Or did she feel that way because she was jealous? No, she couldn't be—she barely knew the man.

'You're very quiet, Sarah.'

She looked up, startled at suddenly being drawn into the conversation. But she should have known Griff wouldn't let her just sit back unnoticed.

She gave him an over-bright smile, aware that Clarissa was giving her a slightly indignant look, that Sally's gaze was openly resentful. When she would much rather have been left out of the conversation herself, it was ludicrous that the other two women should react so antagonistically.

'It's been a full day,' she excused her quietness.

'How nice.' Sally looked at her interestedly. 'What did you and Daddy do this afternoon?'

Sarah gave a puzzled frown. 'I spent the afternoon in the pool with Stephen; I'm not sure what your father was doing...'

'Sleeping, actually,' Roger put in drily, with a meaningful look at his wife.

'And Ben?' Sally continued in that light conversational tone. 'Did he spend the afternoon at the pool with you—and Stephen?'

Why was Sally behaving so oddly? What did she mean by the conversation? She surely wasn't implying—— No, she couldn't be!

'Coffee, anyone?' Clarissa suggested, standing up, drawing the attention back to herself, looking beautiful in a fitted red dress that somehow made her hair look deeply auburn. 'Stephen, it's time you went to bed,' she told him lightly. 'No arguments, darling,' she added firmly as he would have protested. 'You know what the deal was.'

'But——'

'I'll take him through,' Roger offered, standing up to talk softly to Stephen as he protested loudly all the way to his bedroom.

'Coffee, Griff?' Clarissa's voice had lowered huskily.

'Thanks.' He nodded easy acceptance, standing up to come around the table and pull back Sarah's chair for her. 'I enjoyed the meal very much, thank you,' he told her warmly.

Sarah shot an uncomfortable glance around the table, relieved to see that Clarissa had already gone through to the kitchen to make the coffee, that Roger had returned to the room and was in conversation with Ben. Only Sally watched them with narrowed eyes.

Sarah hastily led the way through to the sitting area. 'This isn't wise,' she muttered for Griff alone.

'I want to talk to you,' he told her softly. 'Why else do you think I came to dinner at all?'

'Because you were asked,' she snapped.

'Because I wanted to see you,' he corrected in a low voice.

Sarah turned to him sharply, shaking her head at the warmth of his gaze. 'Griff, I——'

'Do you realise that's the first time you've called me by my name?' he cut in gruffly.

Delicate colour entered her cheeks. 'This afternoon was a mistake——'

'No mistake, Sarah,' he cut in firmly. 'A little ill-timed, perhaps, but——'

'Come on, Ben.' Sally spoke loudly enough for them to hear her. 'Let's join Sarah and Griff.'

'That young lady is going to get her bottom smacked before very long,' Griff muttered for Sarah alone.

She gave a rueful smile. 'She would probably enjoy it!'

'No doubt,' he muttered again. 'But I am going to talk to you, Sarah,' he warned softly. 'So stop avoiding me.'

Her eyes flashed a warning. 'As soon as you stop making things difficult for me here!'

'Sarah——'

'Did you finish your work today, Griff?' Sally interrupted challengingly.

'Later,' he promised Sarah before turning to face Sally, his gaze steady. 'As a matter of fact, I did get some work done today,' he nodded.

'Work?' Roger repeated in a puzzled voice. 'But I thought you were here because——'

'Shall I make room on the table for you?' Sarah offered thankfully as Clarissa came through with the tray of coffee; really, were all of this family lacking in tact?

'I'm actually trying to write a book,' Griff answered Roger while Sarah hastily cleared the coffee-table, although she turned to him sharply when he said this. 'I'm not doing too well,' he added ruefully. 'Writing a book isn't as easy as I thought it would be.'

'But that's so interesting.' Clarissa sat down, crossing one slender leg over the other, showing off a long expanse of bare, tanned thigh. 'What's the book about?' she encouraged as she began to pour the coffee for them all.

Sarah sat back on her heels, listening intently to what Griff was saying. As far as she was aware, he had never written a book before—at least, she had never seen one with the name Griff Morgan as author. But, then, perhaps he had a pseudonym?

Griff shrugged. 'I'm not sure yet—that's part of the problem I'm having with it.' He gave a self-derisive smile.

'Sarah, take this coffee over to Griff.' Clarissa held out the cup to her.

She got up automatically to do as she was instructed, but Sally got there before her, almost knocking her over as she grabbed the cup of coffee and turned towards Griff.

'Sally!' Roger looked at his daughter exasperatedly, the deliberate rudeness too obvious to go unchecked, shaking his head at Griff as their gazes met in complete understanding.

Sarah stepped back, not in the least put out, interested in this book Griff was writing in spite of herself. 'Does this mean we won't be seeing any more of your exposé stories in the newspapers?'

'Er—not for a while, anyway,' he confirmed a little restrainedly.

Of course! Until Saturday Griff had been working for Sandra's father on his newspaper; that could be a little awkward for all of them now that Sandra had decided not to marry Griff.

'A book about the adventures you've encountered while working on your stories would be fascinating.' Roger nodded interestedly.

Griff frowned. 'I had something more in the fiction line in mind.'

'I'm sure it will be wonderful, whatever you decide to do,' Clarissa told him brightly. 'We'll be sure to look out for it.'

Griff sat down, smiling slightly. 'Oh, it wouldn't be published for months after I've completed it—whenever that might be.' He grimaced. 'This delay in publishing is something else I would have to get used to; I'm accustomed to a more immediate market.'

'What made you decide on the change?' Roger queried curiously.

Sarah had a feeling it might not have been completely Griff's decision, that he might not actually have been given any choice.

'It was time for a change.' Griff shrugged dismissively. 'Unfortunately, the pool is becoming a temptation I'm finding hard to resist.'

Sally looked at him coyly. 'Only the pool?'

Sarah felt the colour flood into her cheeks as Griff looked not at Sally but at her, albeit almost against his will.

And she was far from the only one to notice the way he turned to her.

Clarissa watched them with raised brows, obviously deeply curious.

Ben's gaze narrowed suspiciously.

Roger looked slightly puzzled.

But it was Sally, the one who had initiated the flirtation, who looked absolutely furious.

Sarah knew that look only too well, and she tensed for the retaliation.

It wasn't long in coming!

'Sarah's enjoying her stay here too, aren't you?' Sally prompted brittly.

Where was this conversation going to go? 'Well—I——'

'But then, with all these lovely men around, she would, wouldn't she?' Sally continued tauntingly.

'Sal——'

'Oh, stop acting so outraged, Mummy.' She turned on Clarissa as she would have rebuked her. 'You can't have been blind to the way Sarah has been flirting with Daddy, and Ben, and——'

'That's a lie!' Sarah gasped incredulously. Ben had been making a nuisance of himself, and as for Roger——

'—and we all know that Sarah only came away with us at all to get away from the scandal she caused in England,' Sally concluded scornfully, standing up to look down triumphantly at a now white-faced Sarah.

How did Sally know about that? Who could have told——? Sarah heaved a ragged sigh as she saw the impatient fury on Clarissa's face as she looked at her daughter, knowing she needed look no further for Sally's source. And she didn't need two guesses who had talked to Clarissa about her completely personal business. Clarissa's good friend, Sarah's own mother! It explained so much—even this unexpected suggestion that she come away with the Forbes family in the first place. Oh, Mother!

She hardly dared look at Griff, and when she did his expression told her none of his feelings, although he now sat tensely forward on his chair where minutes before he had been relaxing back in it.

Well, that was hardly surprising; he must be wondering what sort of scandal she was running away from!

'Sally, I think it might be best if you go to your room,' Roger told his daughter tautly, all of the paternal indulgence for her earlier behaviour completely gone.

'But——'

'Go—to—your—room!' he thundered at her this time, his usually mild temperament pushed to its limit.

Sally looked at them all, appealing for someone to back her up. No one appeared to be about to do so in the face of this uncharacteristic anger from Roger, even Clarissa, for once, silent.

Tears filled Sally's eyes before she gave a choked sob and ran from the room.

Sarah felt an urgent need to escape too, standing up abruptly.

'Sarah,' Roger touched her arm, 'I'm so sorry about what Sally just said. I don't know how she came to know so much about your personal business, but I——'

'Oh, don't be ridiculous, Roger,' Clarissa scorned impatiently, her silence at an end. 'I suppose she overheard Margaret and me talking about it,' she dismissed.

Just as Sarah had thought. Oh, Mother; she gave an inward groan at this apparent disloyalty, although she was sure her mother had only done it at the time because she was so worried about Sarah. But wasn't it enough that she had to live with her mistake—did everyone else have to know about it too?

'Then the two of you had no right letting her overhear you,' Roger turned on Clarissa.

She looked furious at this public rebuke. 'We were only telling the truth,' she defended indignantly. 'And, anyway, I don't know why you should suddenly be so protective of Sarah. Unless...?' She looked at the two of them suspiciously.

'I'm going for a walk,' Sarah cut in tautly.

Clarissa's eyes were narrowed to hard blue slits. '*Has* something been going on between the two of you behind my back?' she demanded to know. 'After all,' she added hardly, 'Sarah has done her best to break up one marriage; why should another one matter to her?'

Roger drew in a sharp, controlling breath. 'If anyone succeeds in breaking up our marriage it will be you, Clarissa, with your bitchiness!' He shook his head. 'I came away for a rest, a holiday, and instead of relaxing as I'd expected it's been one late night after another, so that I hardly have the strength to make love to *you*, let alone another woman! As for Sarah, she's been treated more like a slave than a friend of the family doing us a favour by helping us out, the way that she was supposed to be!'

'Sally was right about that,' Clarissa told him waspishly. 'If it weren't for the scandal Sarah had caused for herself in England she wouldn't have come away with us at all!'

'After the way she's been treated, I'm sure she wishes she had never bothered,' Roger said exasperatedly, which started a verbal tirade from Clarissa that seemed in danger of never stopping.

Sarah *wished* she could walk out of here and never come back, but something had happened to her legs, so that she couldn't seem to move them. But she felt like a particularly nasty insect put on display, everyone seeming to be staring at her when she needed so desperately to get away.

'Come on.' Griff gently took hold of her arm.

She looked up at him as if she had never seen him before.

'We're leaving,' he told Clarissa and Roger loud enough to interrupt their argument.

Clarissa brought herself under control with effort, slowly realising what she had done, and in front of someone like Griff Morgan. 'There's no need for you to go. Either of you,' she added hastily as she saw the proprietorial hold Griff had of Sarah's arm. 'This is just a little misunderstanding——'

'I don't think so,' Griff cut in calmly as he felt the tremor that passed through Sarah. 'Thank you,' he added tautly. 'Sarah?' He indicated she should leave ahead of him.

She walked across the room, her head held high as she saw Ben was looking at her with a sly reassessment she found repellent, obviously unaware of the reason she hadn't minded leaving England for a few weeks until a couple of minutes ago, Clarissa's gaze furious at having her guest whisked away from under her nose in this way, and Roger watching her with open respect. But, even so, Sarah had no doubt he would be made to pay for his defence of her once she and Griff had left!

She breathed in deep gulps of warm fresh air once they were outside, the feeling of oppression instantly beginning to fade, although she still felt unclean from the accusations that had been hurled at her.

All the more so because what had been said about Simon was mostly true. She had broken up his marriage, caused a scandal that had reverberated around the hospital where they both worked. It didn't matter that the relationship was over, that she had probably lost her chance of promotion because of it, that Simon was even now trying to patch up his marriage; she had been branded the selfish little bitch chasing after a married man, and it did no good, she knew from experience, to cry her innocence.

And Griff had been a witness to the accusations of her shame. What must he think of her?

She looked at him tentatively in the darkness.

'I don't think anything,' he sighed, correctly reading her thoughts—once again. 'Except possibly to pity Roger Forbes for the wife and family he has.' Griff shook his head. 'I would want to strangle the lot of them!'

'It was true, you know. What they said,' she added as Griff looked unmoved. 'All of it.' She shuddered, remembering all too well the awkwardness and terrible embarrassment there had been at the hospital once her relationship with Simon had become public knowledge. Somehow the 'other woman', as she had become known, seemed to come out the worst in these things, the man seeming to be thought an innocent victim of her machinations.

That was far from the truth in this case!

'Let's go for a drive,' Griff said firmly as the raised voices of Clarissa and Roger could clearly be heard from inside the villa.

'Griff, I said——'

'I heard what you said.' He turned to her intently. '*I* said, let's go for a drive.'

He guided her firmly over to his car, seeing her safely seated inside before going around the other side to get in behind the wheel.

They didn't talk; Griff just drove away from the villa, out of the village, and up into the mountains. Not far up, he stopped the car in an almost empty car park that belonged to a restaurant, their view over the village and the valley around it.

And still they didn't talk, both of them lost in their own thoughts.

Sarah cringed at what Griff's must be about!

It had all started out so innocently. Simon had been new to the hospital, all the female staff falling for his blond-haired Adonis looks. But of them all he had chosen Sarah to ask out.

She had been flattered, excited, that first date passing in a perfect dream.

They had been seeing each other on a fairly regular basis when he'd told her his wife was due back that evening so he wouldn't be able to see her until tomorrow.

Wife!

Back from *where*?

The grapevine hadn't been sure whether Simon was married or not when he'd first come to the hospital; some had said yes, some had said no, but the general consensus had seemed to be that Simon had been married once but was now separated or divorced.

And they had all been wrong.

Simon was still very much married—had actually been taking Sarah out during the time that his wife had been away on holiday.

And now she'd been coming back.

It was an unhappy marriage, Simon had claimed when Sarah had confronted him with the deception. And anyway, he'd told her, he hadn't set out to deceive her at all; she had just never asked if he was married or not. That this was true didn't alter the unpalatable fact that she had fallen in love with a married man.

His marriage was all a sham, he'd told her, held together by their ten-year-old daughter, neither one of them wanting to hurt the one good thing to come out of their marriage. As soon as Melissa was old enough——

And when did he expect that to be, Sarah had asked with sarcasm—when she was eighteen, twenty-one, when she married? But then there would be grandchildren, and they couldn't be hurt either, could they?

Simon had seemed heartbroken by her anger, asked, *begged* for her understanding, claiming he couldn't lose her now that he had found her.

It had all sounded so convincing.

And she had been so stupid.

So naïve.

And it didn't help in the least that she was far from the first woman to fall for that 'my wife doesn't understand me' line. *She* should have known better, shouldn't have been swayed by a love that was doomed from the onset. And not only because Simon was already married.

Through it all she hadn't noticed, or realised, that not once had Simon said that he loved her and wanted to be with her!

And that was because, as she had later discovered, he had been lying to her about the state of his marriage. His marriage to Fiona was no worse than a lot of fifteen-year marriages that had slipped into complacency.

Simon had certainly had no intention of ever stepping out of it, had been quite happy with the comfort of his wife at home and Sarah to add excitement to his life at work and on the evenings they did manage to grab a few hours together.

And then his wife, on her way to a night out with some girlfriends, had seen the two of them drinking together in a pub. Why wasn't Simon at his staff-meeting? Fiona had wanted to know, still completely innocent of what she had really stumbled upon. Sarah was one of his staff, Simon had claimed, and as the meeting had finished early they had decided to have a drink before going home.

Sarah had been mortified at the meeting. All these weeks 'Fiona' had been a shadowy figure who made Simon unhappy, but, actually coming face to face with this tall raven-haired woman who was beautiful enough to have been a model, Sarah had suddenly felt inadequate and used.

And still Fiona had remained blind to what they were really doing there together, but, as she'd continued to talk to them brightly, understanding had slowly begun to dawn on her, and she'd looked from Sarah's awkward embarrassment back to Simon's over-jolly mood in disbelief.

Sarah hoped she never again had to witness the crumbling of another woman's total trust in her husband, her secure if complacent world disintegrating in front of her eyes.

Fiona had told Simon she thought it best if they discussed this when they got home, and Sarah had offered no objection when Simon had said he thought he ought to leave with his wife now. As far as she, Sarah, was concerned, the myth of her relationship was finally over.

But now Simon's marriage really was in a shambles, and he had relied on Sarah's friendship more than ever as Fiona, humiliated beyond endurance, had broadcast far and wide that Sarah and Simon had been having an affair.

In the midst of all the gossip and whispering that had spread through the hospital like wildfire, Sarah had felt she didn't have any other friend but Simon she could talk to. And he was far from ideal!

But Fiona Robbins hadn't finished yet, had seen to it that Sarah's private life wasn't thought respectable enough for a new ward sister, and Sarah's hopes of getting the post vanished into thin air. She thought about starting afresh somewhere else.

As for Simon and Fiona, they would get over this little set-back, he'd assured Sarah; things would settle down again, and then they could all get on with their lives as before.

Sarah had known then that he would never leave his wife, had never intended to, that, for all his protestations to the contrary, for all that he was attracted to Sarah, he loved Fiona and would never end his marriage to her.

Sarah had taken immediate leave from the hospital, needing this break to try and sort out what she should do with her life now.

She had had no idea that the Forbes family knew anything about that tangled mess she had left behind, certainly hadn't expected to have it thrown up at her as an accusation accompanying implications that she had been flirting with Roger and Ben since they had been here!

There was no way she could return to the Forbes villa after that.

She turned from staring sightlessly over the valley with its scattering of twinkling lights from the villas hidden among the many trees, looking at Griff in the darkness. 'I can't go back there,' she stated flatly.

He returned her gaze steadily, as if he had been waiting until she felt able to talk. 'No,' he acknowledged gruffly.

She suddenly broke down in the darkness, burying her face in her hands. 'What am I going to do?' she cried.

Griff didn't hesitate. 'You're going to come back to Virginia's villa and stay the night with me.'

CHAPTER SIX

SARAH became very still, her hands falling slowly down from in front of her face as she looked at Griff with pained eyes. 'Just because Clarissa claimed I broke a man's marriage up doesn't mean that I——'

'Don't, Sarah,' Griff warned harshly. 'The offer was—although perhaps I didn't make myself completely clear—for you to stay the night at Virginia's villa with me, but certainly not in the same bedroom.'

She swallowed hard, knowing from Griff's expression that he was angry about the assumption she had made. 'I'm sorry.' She drew in a ragged breath. 'It's no excuse, but I was just so upset——'

'Of course it's not an excuse,' Griff dismissed impatiently. 'It's a damned good reason. How the hell you stuck it out with that rabid family as long as you did is beyond me!'

She gave a faint, humourless smile. 'I thought I was doing them a good turn.'

He raised his brows scathingly. 'One they obviously didn't appreciate.'

She blinked back the sudden tears. 'I can't believe that all the time they were thinking that of me.' She shook her head. 'Not that it isn't true, but——' She broke off as Griff's hand covered both of hers as she moved them restlessly in her lap, looking across at him uncertainly.

He gave a rueful shrug. 'As I tried to explain to you yesterday—— No, don't, Sarah.' His hand tightened on hers as she would have pulled away at this reminder of the kiss they had shared. 'Things aren't always what they seem,' he repeated firmly. 'Or what people say they are.'

As Simon's marriage hadn't been the sham he had claimed it was!

'No,' she agreed heavily.

Griff looked at her closely, seeing the emotional exhaustion on her face, releasing her hands to briskly restart the car. 'What we are going to do now is go back to the villa, have a cup of hot chocolate for you—no, not the "Morgan coffee",' he added self-derisively as he drove the car back on the road. 'The idea is to help you get to sleep, not keep you awake! I'll be having a glass of whisky myself. And then we're both going to get an early night.'

'But——'

'Sleep, Sarah,' he insisted firmly. 'It's the best thing for you right now.'

She did feel shattered, but she wasn't sure she would be able to sleep. Everything seemed to have exploded in her face yet again, and she wasn't sure how she was going to get away from it this time.

Griff glanced at her. 'Don't worry,' he instructed briskly. 'Worrying never solved anything.'

Neither did sitting back and doing nothing, she wanted to tell him. But she was too exhausted even to argue with him, quietly withdrawn on the short drive back, sitting in the lounge when he told her to while he went into the kitchen to get their drinks. She even drank the hot chocolate automatically, barely tasting it, wondering if she was going to go on paying for the nightmare of her mistake, that of loving the wrong man, for the rest of her life.

Griff took one look at her face once she had finished her drink and firmly announced, 'Bed!'

He showed her into the second spare room. Well, he didn't so much show her as steer her in the right direction, her movements like an automaton still, although she knew the bedroom from her previous visits here.

'I'll go and get you one of Virginia's nightgowns to sleep in,' Griff told her gently. 'Although,' he added with a grimace, 'her night attire, believe it or not, tends to run towards the exotic.'

Thinking of the meticulously turned-out Virginia Majors, no matter what the occasion, she decided that Griff's rueful attitude towards his sister's night attire was understandable. Somehow she couldn't see the other woman in exotic underwear either. But then her judgement of people wasn't too *good* at the moment . . .

She was still sitting on the side of the pink floral-covered duvet when Griff returned from his sister's room, her eyes widening at the silky black nightgown he had draped over one arm, standing up slowly.

He made a face as he saw her expression. 'Virginia doesn't believe pale colours suit her blonde colouring,' he explained with a shrug, putting the silk garment down on the bed to thrust his hands into his trouser pockets.

The other woman probably knew best what suited her, and Sarah was certainly in no position to question her taste. 'It doesn't matter,' she dismissed. 'I had better get to bed,' she sighed, touching the gown despondently.

Griff straightened, taking his hands out of his pockets to take a step towards her.

Sarah flinched.

She couldn't help it; this man had shown her nothing but kindness, and yet she had flinched none the less.

He came to an abrupt halt, his expression softening as he looked down at her bent head. 'I'm just going to help you take your hair down,' he explained softly. 'And then you can get undressed and into bed, and get some sleep.'

She was too numb to stop him as he gently sat her down before quietly beginning to loosen her hair from its plait, running his fingers through the silken blonde tresses as he fanned them out over her shoulders.

'I know this isn't the time,' he spoke gruffly, 'and I'm certainly not going to take advantage of your situation, but I need you to know how very much I want to kiss you again!'

Sarah looked up at him, startled green eyes looking straight into honey-brown.

'Oh, Sarah...!' he groaned, pulling her gently to her feet and gathering her close against his chest, enveloped by his warmth.

She was trembling badly, clinging to him, wanting the nightmare to end. But it never seemed to...

Gentle lips travelled the long length of her throat, nuzzling against the lobe of her ear, teeth lightly biting before his mouth continued the path along her jaw and at last found the parted, waiting softness of her lips.

It wasn't passion they shared but understanding, Griff giving Sarah at that moment all the comfort and assurance that she needed.

But as their kisses deepened and lengthened desire leapt between them, Griff's hands moving restlessly over her back and waist as he moulded her to the length of his body.

Hot breaths mingled, Griff's lips capturing, searching, demanding.

Sarah met that demand, her arms up about his neck, moving sensuously against him, her body afire, her breasts aching, springing to life as a thumb moved lightly over its tip, hardening with a need that Griff was only too happy to assuage, his lips travelling the length of her throat now to close over that hardened nipple through the thin material of her dress.

Sensations unlike any she had ever known before blazed through her body, her throat arching as her head fell back languidly, the warm caress of Griff's tongue moving to her other straining breast, the nipple already perked temptingly for his moist caress.

She had lost all thought, all need, other than knowing the full possession of Griff's body as he moved so longingly against her, the warmth at her thighs becoming a physical ache as Griff moved his hardness against her, his hands on her thighs as he held her to him.

Her eyes were dark with need as he lay her back on the bed, offering no resistance as he lowered the zip to her dress and drew the garment away from her altogether, leaving her clothed only in a pair of black lace briefs.

Griff looked down at her with eyes the colour of gold. 'You're beautiful,' he groaned hungrily, slowly caressing her. 'Absolutely lovely to behold,' he told her huskily.

She felt beautiful with him, unashamedly beautiful in her nakedness. 'Make love to me, Griff,' she invited softly.

He swallowed hard. 'I want that so badly that I ache with it,' he told her shakily. 'But I don't want to do anything tonight that you're going to hate me for in the morning.' His voice was ragged with emotion.

Reality came back like a cold slap in the face, and she stared up at him, the horror in her eyes for her wanton behaviour of a few minutes ago.

What must he think of her? Oh, God, after this he couldn't help but believe all that Sally and Clarissa had said about her!

She rolled over on her side, turned away from him, her face buried hotly in the pillow.

'Sarah, no!' Griff clasped the warmth of her bare shoulders between firm hands, but she wouldn't be turned towards him.

'You'll believe them now,' she choked. 'Believe I'm a flirt, a home-wrecker, a——'

'No!' he protested harshly. 'You're a warm, vibrant woman, and I know you well enough to realise you would never set out to hurt anyone willingly. You fell in love with this man——'

'I *thought* I loved Simon,' she cut in raggedly, still turned away from him, realising even as she said the words that she no longer loved Simon, if she ever had.

At first Simon had seemed so exciting to be with, an elusive consultant, and then when she had discovered he was married she had believed him when he'd said it was unhappily, had felt sorry for him when he'd told her how awful his life with Fiona was, and now . . . God, *now* she had met a man she could so easily love, and it was all so terribly wrong. The wrong time, the wrong place, *everything*!

'We all make mistakes, Sarah,' Griff told her regretfully. 'But we don't have to go on paying for them for the rest of our lives.'

Oh, God, she had forgotten, however briefly, that less than a week ago this man had been left standing at thc altar by the woman he loved!

'I—— Thank you for helping me tonight.' She drew in a deep controlling breath. 'I think I would like to get some sleep now.' She kept her eycs firmly closed, knowing that to open them and look into his dear face could be her undoing.

His hands were slowly removed from her shoulders, the skin there suddenly feeling chill, and Sarah didn't see him but she felt him move from the side of the bed, heard the click of the bedroom door as he opened it seconds later, her nerves stretched to breaking-point almost by this time.

She could feel him watching her, before he called to her softly, 'Night, Sarah.'

'Goodnight.' She tried to sound casual, and groaned inwardly as she was sure she only managed to sound offhand.

'Nothing has changed, Sarah,' he told her softly. 'I still like you, respect you—and want you so badly that it's actually a physical pain!'

By the time she had turned to face him he had gone, the bedroom door closing softly behind him.

The tears began to fall hotly, scalding her cheeks, and she knew she no longer cried for Simon and their lost love.

Because she *had* never loved him, only thought she had, she was sure of that now.

Griff Morgan was the man she loved!

She awoke to the bright south of France sun shining through her bedroom curtains; there was nothing unusual about that.

But it was the only thing this morning that was the same as the previous twelve days.

On those previous mornings there had been no delicious smell of freshly brewed coffee drifting through the villa to her bedroom—she'd always been the one who'd got up and made coffee for everyone else!

And she could smell hot bread and pastries too—no one got those either normally until she had driven down to the village bakery to pick up the fresh long sticks of bread, still warm from the oven and the assorted pastries.

And the silk she could feel against her skin wasn't the usual cotton nightshirt she wore.

And the person whistling noisily outside her bedroom door couldn't be one of the Forbes family—they were all alike in one way, and that was that none of them was cheerful in the morning.

And the Forbeses certainly didn't have a cat that could have made itself comfortable at the bottom of her bed so that it made it difficult for her to stretch out!

'Up you sit,' Griff ordered as he let himself into the room after the briefest of knocks, pushing the cat off the bed before putting a laden tray down in front of Sarah with a flourish as she scrambled hastily up the bed into a sitting position, more out of a feeling of awkwardness than to actually do what he instructed.

'Coffee—weak, in your honour,' he added teasingly. 'Fresh fruit juice. Orange. Freshly squeezed by my own fair hand. Bread, still warm from the oven, soft butter, marmalade, and delicious pastries,' he triumphantly announced the contents of the tray. 'You know,' he sat down on the side of the bed, helping himself to one of the pastries, a lovely concoction of almonds and glacé cherries on top of the soft pastry, 'I could quite get used to bringing you breakfast in bed.'

Well, he wasn't about to be given the chance; she would have to leave here. And as soon as possible. As soon as she had at least made an attempt to eat some of the breakfast he had prepared so nicely for her; she couldn't disappoint him when he had taken so much trouble for her, couldn't remember anyone else ever doing such a thing, not even her parents.

'I shouldn't,' she told him drily, breaking open some of the bread, hungry in spite of herself at its deliciously tempting smell, spreading on some of the golden butter. 'I shall be leaving as soon as I've booked my flight home to England.'

All the laughter left Griff's face at this announcement. 'You don't have to do that,' he protested. 'You could stay on here and have a holiday——'

'No, I couldn't,' Sarah said firmly, knowing that wouldn't be a good idea in the circumstances. And he had to know it too. After last night.

Last night ...

She suddenly lost all taste for the bread she had buttered so enthusiastically seconds earlier. Last night she had wanted Griff to make love to her, had wanted him as badly as he had claimed to want her, could still remember the warmth of his lips on her body.

Last night she had realised she loved this man ...

Griff's hand covered hers as he watched the emotions flickering across her face. 'Sarah, we have to talk——'

'No!' She pulled away from him, putting the tray firmly to one side to throw back the bedclothes and leap out of the bed.

The thought of putting on the black dress she had worn the evening before was distasteful to her; she doubted she would ever be able to wear that particular dress again without remembering her humiliation of last night. But the only alternative seemed to be the revealing black nightgown.

She snatched up the black dress from the bedroom chair where Griff seemed to have draped it some time after getting up from the bed and before leaving the room the night before, hurrying into the adjoining bathroom.

Her reflection in the bathroom mirror showed her face to be pale, with dark shadows under over-big green eyes. It had taken her hours to fall asleep last night, her sleep filled with dreams when she had eventually managed to drop off.

She dressed quickly, relieved to see Griff had gone when she returned to the bedroom, tidying the bed, laying the silk nightgown across the bottom of the bed, Jasper having wandered off, in search of food probably.

But she would have to find Griff and thank him for his help before she left.

She found him in the kitchen when she took the tray through, the debris from the oranges he had squeezed, the coffee he had made, and the bread he had broken up into more manageable pieces still evident in the untidiness of the room. Griff stood unconcernedly in the middle of it, his hand arrested in raising his coffee-mug to his lips, his piercing gaze fixed on Sarah.

'Thank you for coming to my rescue last night.' She attempted a brightness she didn't feel, pleased when she managed to sound quite natural, although all the same she lacked conviction. 'I'm going to collect my things now, and——'

'I'm coming with you.'

Her eyes widened at the flat determination in his voice, his eyes narrowed challengingly. 'I can manage——'

'I'm sure you can.' He gave an acknowledging inclination of his head. 'I'm still coming with you.' He met her gaze steadily.

Sarah returned that gaze impatiently, knowing that if she told him he wasn't coming with her he was more than likely to follow her anyway. And that would look worse than if they went together in the first place!

'Very well—as you insist,' she accepted abruptly. 'But it's a waste of your time. I only intend collecting my things and going straight to the airport. I shall just camp out there until I can get a flight home,' she added with more bravado than she actually felt, knowing that getting a seat on a flight to England could be difficult at this time of year.

Although, at the moment, facing the Forbes family again was most prominent in her thoughts!

It was just her luck that the family were at the dining table having breakfast—at least, Roger and the three children were, Sarah's gaze moving to the kitchen doorway where a harassed-looking Clarissa now stood, her hair not in its usually perfect style, her face bare of make-up; she looked all of her forty-three years this morning.

Sarah didn't fool herself into thinking that Clarissa's less than perfect turn-out this morning had anything to do with being upset by the scene with her the night before; it was more likely to be because she was having to do some of the housework herself for a change!

'There are only cereals and toast for breakfast this morning,' her disgruntled words to the family seemed to confirm this, 'so you will have to make do with——' Clarissa broke off the speech, having realised that none of her family was taking the slightest bit of notice of her, that they had their attention fixed on something across the room. She followed their gaze. 'Sarah...!' she breathed slowly.

'Where have you been?' Stephen demanded. 'Breakfast sounds awful. Sally's been mean to me. And your bed wasn't slept in last night,' he accused indignantly, obviously upset at having his comfortable routine put out in this way.

'Stephen!' Clarissa glared at her youngest offspring, glancing uncomfortably at Griff as he stood slightly behind Sarah across the room.

'Well, it wasn't,' he added rebelliously, determined to have the last word.

'Stephen...' his father spoke quietly, but with a steely quality in his voice that couldn't be ignored, even by his younger son, Stephen looking up at him with widely surprised eyes. '...shut up,' Roger told him coldly.

Sarah felt more uncomfortable than ever in the black dress after the exchange!

'I'm not staying,' she assured them all drily, her gaze scathing as it rested on each of them in turn.

Stephen still looked rebellious from his father's rebuke, but was silent none the less, Sally had a secretive little smile playing about her lips, Ben was looking questioningly from Sarah to Griff and then back again, Roger looked uncomfortable with the whole situation, and Clarissa looked—it was difficult to tell how

Clarissa looked; she seemed flustered, completely unlike herself.

Sarah frowned.

'You may have to,' Clarissa told her in a harassed voice.

Sarah shook her head. 'I'll get a flight back to England some time, and until I do I'll find somewhere in Nice to stay.'

'That isn't what I meant at all,' Clarissa told her restlessly. 'Oh, this is so awful! Roger, do *something*! What am I going to tell Margaret?' she added with a distressed wail.

There was no doubting that Sarah's mother would be upset at this rift between her daughter and her oldest friend, but Sarah felt sure they could all smooth it over somehow.

'Leave that to me,' she assured softly.

Clarissa put up a hand to her untidy red hair, shaking her head. 'You don't understand.'

Sarah's frown deepened. Clarissa certainly hadn't seemed this upset last night.

'Sarah...' Roger stood up, crossing the room to stand in front of her. He briefly chewed on his bottom lip as he glanced at the stony-faced man standing to the side of Sarah, his expression one of appeal as he turned back to Sarah. 'Last night, after you had gone,' he paused

awkwardly, breathing deeply, 'Clarissa realised—discovered,' he amended as his wife gave
a tiny gasp, 'that her diamond bracelet was
missing.' The last came out in a rush, Roger
looking slightly nauseous now.

Sarah knew the bracelet he was talking about;
Clarissa wore it most evenings when she went
out, a large garish affair of gold and diamonds
that must have cost a small fortune.

No wonder Clarissa looked harassed this
morning!

'We haven't called in the police,' Roger added
uncomfortably. 'We're going to have a good
look around the villa for it first, with your help,
hopefully, and trust that it—turns up.' He
shifted awkwardly, his dismissive shrug not
quite coming off, looking sicker than ever, his
face pale.

Sarah looked wordlessly from the gaunt-faced
Clarissa to Roger, who looked more stricken
than anything else.

Stephen watched her with mouth agape; Sally
looked at her challengingly; Ben didn't seem to
know where to look.

Sarah turned back to Clarissa and Roger,
didn't need for either of them to say that when
they hoped the bracelet would 'turn up' what

they really meant was they hoped the diamond bracelet would be returned to them without any more fuss.

They both thought *she* had taken it!

CHAPTER SEVEN

'SMUG-FACED little——' Griff broke off furiously. 'I'd like to have——'

'Roger wasn't smug at all,' Sarah said dully. 'Of them all he looked the most upset.'

'I wasn't talking about him,' Griff grated contemptuously. 'The daughter looked like the proverbial cat that got the cream,' he recalled grimly.

The last half an hour had been a nightmare—when hadn't this working holiday, one way or another?

There could be no question of her leaving France now, not until the bracelet had been found. To do so, Sarah felt, would only add to the conviction the Forbes family seemed to have that she was the guilty one. Her claim that she didn't even *like* the bracelet that had gone missing had been dealt with by Sally, who had pointed out she could have taken the bracelet out of spite.

That had been when Griff had stepped in!

He had been remarkably controlled during the exchange, but this last bit had been too much for him, telling the Forbeses that she was leaving with him once she had packed her clothes, that she wouldn't be helping them look for anything, they could do their own dirty work, that Sarah could be contacted at the neighbouring villa if absolutely necessary, but that the next time they spoke to her it had better be with an apology first, otherwise none of them had better come near her at all!

Sarah had been choked with emotion at his absolute faith in her innocence. He didn't really know her that well, after all, and even someone who did know her, given the circumstancial evidence—that of the bracelet's having disappeared at the same time as she had stormed out—could be forgiven for doubting her.

Not that she thought she would really have forgiven them, but it gave her a warm glow inside to know that Griff hadn't even hesitated in his total belief in her.

She didn't know how she could have coped with her packing and leaving the Forbes villa without his help, Griff keeping all the family at bay while she'd got her things together, Sarah very careful not to leave anything of hers behind; she had no intention of coming near this family again if she could prevent it!

She had been shaking so badly by the time she'd left that without Griff's hand under her arm she'd felt as if she might have collapsed, grateful for his help in getting into the car too, her gaze fixed rigidly in front of her as they'd driven out of the driveway.

'In fact,' Griff added slowly as they turned in at his sister's villa, 'I wouldn't be at all surprised if Sally didn't have something to do with the missing bracelet herself.'

Sarah frowned as she looked at him. 'Surely not...?' she protested, and yet Sally's triumphant look last night and the smug look on her face this morning came to mind.

'Why not?' Griff challenged, parking the car. 'She was willing to go to any lengths last night to try and discredit you, so why should she stop at theft?' He looked grim.

Put like that, it did sound possible, but... Surely Sally didn't dislike her *that* much?

Griff's face was still grim as he opened the car door for her to get out. 'Let's hope Roger Forbes realises what a vicious little madam his daughter is, before she causes real damage.'

The missing bracelet felt like a dark shadow hanging over Sarah, and the thought of staying here with Griff, after her response to him last night, filled her with trepidation. She didn't seem to have any control over her emotions where this man was concerned, knew without a doubt that the two of them would become lovers if she stayed on here with him.

But the thought of finding somewhere on her own with this sword hanging over her head just waiting to drop was an unpleasant prospect.

And so she had made no protest when Griff had claimed she would be staying with him.

'Anyway,' he added briskly as he watched the emotions chasing across her face, 'we aren't going to sit around here all day moping.'

Sarah got out of the car to stand beside him in the hot sun. 'We aren't?' she derided drily, knowing her mood was being forced.

'No,' he told her decisively. 'We're going to get our beach things together and go down to Juan-les-Pins.'

She looked up at him with dismay. 'Oh, but——'

'No buts, Sarah,' he cut in firmly, taking her suitcase in one hand and a hold of her arm with the other before walking down to his sister's villa. 'A day out on the beach will do us both good.'

She still held back. 'But your work——'

'Will still be there tomorrow,' he dismissed with a sigh, carrying her suitcase straight through to the bedroom she had used the previous night, depositing it on the floor. 'Actually, that's one of the things I'm finding so difficult about writing a book.' He frowned. 'When I do a story I have a deadline; with writing a book, one you don't yet have a publisher for, you have to exercise so much more self-discipline, because there is no editor in the background telling you to get on with it.'

'*I'm* telling you,' she reminded him drily. 'I know,' she gave a half-smile, 'it isn't the same. Couldn't you . . . sort of make your own deadline inside your head? Give yourself a certain amount of time to get it finished?'

He shrugged. 'I don't seem to be having much luck with that idea at the moment.'

And having her invade his solitude couldn't be helping the situation. But he was adamant that she stay here. And she had to be honest and admit she would rather be here with him than anywhere else. Even if she was sure to get hurt for having been stupid enough to fall in love with him...

'You get your costume,' Griff instructed now. 'I'll get us some extra towels.'

She had thought the emerald-coloured bikini she had with her quite daring when she'd bought it, but on the one trip the family had made to the beach at Juan-les-Pins Clarissa and Sally had gone topless, as so many of the other women on the beach had done too.

Sarah hadn't been that daring.

As she wasn't going to be today either, packing both pieces of the bikini in her beach-bag, Griff waiting in the lounge by the time she joined him.

'I've booked us into a restaurant in the village for dinner tonight,' he informed her as he stowed their things away in the boot of the car.

He hadn't wasted any time, must have made the call during the few minutes she'd looked through her case for her bikini!

'I would have been quite happy to have a sandwich or something at the villa,' she protested.

'We can do that another night,' he dismissed. 'Tonight we'll eat out. You look as if a good rest from any housework wouldn't do you any harm,' he rasped. 'And I intend to see that you get one.'

'But——'

'I told you before,' he glanced at her reprovingly as he drove the car capably along the road towards Nice, 'no buts. Now just sit there and enjoy the drive and stop worrying.'

'Yes, sir,' she derided.

He gave a rueful smile. 'I'm not usually this bossy, but with you I seem to have to be.'

Tears filled her eyes without warning. 'You've been very kind to me——'

'I want to see you happy.' His hand reached out and clasped hers. 'I want all those people just to leave you alone, to see you laughing and talking without the shadow of them hanging over you.'

He knew how she felt without her having to say a word.

This was one of the things that had made her fall in love with him so easily and so quickly, the rapport they seemed to have that enabled him almost to know what she was feeling and thinking before she knew it herself.

It could be disconcerting.

'Forget the lot of them,' he instructed again. 'They're just too ignorant to be of any importance. Besides,' he added lightly, 'the day is young and I am beautiful!' He arched dark brows suggestively.

Sarah couldn't help but laugh as he moved his eyebrows up and down and twiddled an imaginary moustache. 'Oh, Thir Jathper,' she lisped, fluttering her eyelashes at him coyly, 'you're tho tewibly wicked.'

Griff dropped the comic pose with a rueful grimace. 'Actually, you'll find I'm terribly conventional.'

She looked at him with puzzled eyes. What did he mean by *that*?

He didn't seem about to enlighten her, instead launching into a hilarious tale of the time he had found himself stranded on an uninhabited island with his own Man Friday, he and a photographer stuck on the island when rough weather had blown up and made it impossible for the boat to set out to pick them up. His description of how they had finally managed to catch some fish to cook for supper proved to be one of the funniest things Sarah had ever heard.

She wasn't naïve, knew Griff was probably exaggerating slightly in an effort to take her mind off the Forbes family and the missing bracelet, but to a certain degree he succeeded.

How could she help but laugh and enjoy his company when he set out to be so deliberately charming?

There were quite a few people on the beach already when they arrived, the locals at Juan-les-Pins seeming to know that if you didn't get there early enough you couldn't get on one of the colourful mattresses laid out so neatly on the white-gold sand.

Sarah was sure that, if people were asked to pay to lie on a mattress on a beach in England, the only way you could get on to the majority of the beaches here at all, they would be outraged. But in the south of France it was accepted that it was the normal thing to do. And the warm, clear blue-green sea in this area looked much more inviting than any sea Sarah had seen back at home.

So she and Griff paid over their money and were shown to two mattresses at the front of the three rows, the attendant handing them their towels before putting up the umbrella that would shield them from getting too burnt in the extreme heat of midday.

Sarah was a little shy about stripping off in front of Griff, which was a little ridiculous after the little he had seen her in the night before!

But once in her bikini she was a little over-dressed if anything, a number of women on the beach already topless.

'Relax,' Griff told her sleepily as she fidgeted about on the mattress that lay alongside his own, trying to get comfortable, very conscious of the lean length of his body as his tanned skin glistened in the sun from the lotion he had applied liberally seconds earlier.

She was *trying* to relax, but it was a little difficult when she was so aware of him lying beside her, his masculinity a tangible thing.

'I think I'll go for a swim,' she announced abruptly, jumping to her feet.

'Sarah.' The very softness of his voice stopped her flight across the sand to the water.

She turned to look at him, swallowing convulsively, knowing she was behaving foolishly. But that burning ache she had known for him the night before was back, and he wasn't even touching her!

His mouth twisted. 'I'll only throw myself on top of you on a public beach on Saturday,' he drawled. 'And today is Friday!'

She ran into the water, going straight under its warmth in an effort to cool her burning cheeks.

'And today is Friday!'—what must he think of her?

The desire she felt for him must have been obvious in her eyes as she'd looked down at him. Hungrily?

Heatedly? *Desperately?* Oh, God, how could she hide the fact that she wanted him so much?

She watched him from time to time as she swam about languidly in the calm water, her hair slicked back from her face and loose down her back; she hadn't even taken the time to fasten her hair into a plait as she usually did before swimming, in too much of a hurry to get away from Griff and the power his masculinity exerted over her.

Griff lay back on his lounger, eyes closed, showing no interest in the near-naked females around him, although Sarah saw that several of these women deliberately made a point of walking past him, when they had no reason for doing so other than to attract his attention.

None of them succeeded.

Several times he sat up on the mattress, but it was only to seek Sarah out in the water to assure himself of her well-being, giving her an acknowledging wave before settling back again.

Well, at least his behaviour didn't point to his being a womaniser.

Then how was she to explain his undoubted interest in her?

'Lunch.'

She looked up from where she was treading water to find Griff standing only feet away at the water's edge, her breath catching in her throat at the tanned magnificence of him.

'Time for lunch,' he repeated patiently when she made no effort to move out of the water.

She couldn't explain away the attraction between them, could only try to control it, given their living-arrangements.

But it wasn't going to be easy!

'If you don't relax soon you're going to snap in half,' Griff advised drily.

Sarah instantly stopped crumbling the bread roll on her plate, realising as she did so that she had more or less demolished it without actually having made any effort to eat any of it!

But her tension had only increased as the day had progressed, and, now that they were out to dinner, going to bed seemed to be looming up fast. And she was uncertain about what was going to happen then.

She knew what she wanted to happen, but it was still the wrong time, the wrong place—in fact, everything about her and Griff's being together now was wrong, not least of all because it would appear they were both on the rebound. At least Griff was, Sarah in no doubt now that what she had felt for Simon was so shallow, was nothing compared with the overwhelming love she had for Griff. The one certainty she had of that was because she knew if Griff wanted her, even only as a means of helping to ease some of his pain over Sandra Preston's rejection, then she would go to him and offer him that comfort. It was something she had never wanted with Simon, no matter how much he had pressed her to.

But they had both—deliberately so, it seemed to Sarah—not mentioned either Simon or Sandra all day. And now, as they dined together in the comfortable restaurant a short way down the valley from the villa, run by a husband and wife, the husband cooking while the wife helped with the selection of their meal, an awkward silence seemed to have fallen over the two of them.

Hence Sarah's tension had increased.

'Sarah,' Griff's hand closed over her own as it rested on the table-top, 'you're a guest in my sister's home——'

'*She* doesn't know that,' Sarah scorned tautly.

'But I do,' he said firmly. 'And until such time as we manage to untangle all the mess we seem to be caught up in—no, I don't just mean this ridiculous business with the Forbes family,' he clarified as tears welled up in her eyes for the second time today. 'We have a lot of talking to do, a lot of explaining necessary, on both sides,' he added softly. 'And none of that is going to be done overnight. Luckily enough, time seems to be something we have plenty of at the moment. Believe me,' he gave a self-derisive smile, 'that's a luxury for me!'

'And me,' she nodded; when she was at home her work at the hospital kept her very busy.

Griff nodded back. 'And one we shouldn't waste.' He picked up her hand, looking at its capable length, with the fingernails kept deliberately short so that she shouldn't injure any of her patients with them. Griff kissed the fingertips. 'Let's just enjoy this time out of time, and then deal with all the other problems as they arrive, hm?' he encouraged softly.

That had to be easier said than done, given the obstacles they did have. And how was she supposed to relax, when to do that would probably reveal her growing love for this man?

'I don't want to be too late back.' She straightened, releasing her hand. 'I think I should give the Forbeses a ring before I go to bed to see if the bracelet has turned up.'

Griff arched dark brows. 'You don't seriously expect it to have done?' he derided.

She sighed. 'I have to hope it might have done.'

He shook his head. 'Not unless that young lady has had a serious change of heart.'

'We can't be sure——'

'Can't we?' Griff made a face. 'I would say it's a pretty sure bet. But if you want to telephone the Forbeses when we get back I'll go along with that.'

If you want to ruin a perfectly nice day, he didn't say but his tone implied.

And it had been a nice day, eating a deliciously prepared salad for lunch at the beach restaurant only feet away from their mattresses, in a civilised way at a check-tablecloth-covered table rather than sitting on the sand and eating half the beach with the food the way you normally did when eating on a beach.

They had relaxed and dozed in the sun most of the afternoon, only finally moving themselves for the drive back so that they could shower and change before dinner.

But the reality of the missing bracelet wouldn't go away just because they chose to ignore it for a few hours.

'Do you have any close family?' She decided to change the subject altogether, rather than argue with him about it. 'Besides your sister, of course,' she added ruefully, having forgotten that Virginia Major *was* his sister with all that had happened to her since she'd first met him.

He nodded, the expression in his golden-brown eyes telling her that he knew exactly what she was doing, but that he was prepared to go along with it—for the moment. 'The aged Ps live in Devon.'

She smiled. 'I should think they have become even more "aged" than they need have been, worrying about what their son does for a living!'

'My mother, although it isn't widely known, is Barbara Hilliard,' Griff told her with obvious pride in the woman who had become a household name in the fifties for her own adventurous exploits as she too had tracked down stories that no other reporter had seemed able to get.

Sarah looked at him dazedly. 'I had no idea.'

'Most people don't.' He shrugged. 'It was the one thing I insisted upon when I knew I wanted to enter the same profession. I either did it under my own steam through my own ability, or not at all. And, as Mother pretty well dropped out of the reporting world when she gave up journalism, not too many people were ever aware that Barbara Hilliard had a husband and two children.'

'How did your father cope with her profession?' Sarah asked with some interest, knowing that Barbara Hilliard had been one of *the* reporters of her time.

'My father is a doctor,' Griff answered, as if that said everything.

And maybe it did. Doctors, and indeed nurses too, were more aware of the fragility of even normal life, so that the extraordinary was somehow taken in one's stride.

'They're both retired now, of course,' Griff smiled affectionately, 'but still very interesting characters. They would both love to meet you,' he added with certainty.

Sarah gave him a startled look; the chances of her ever meeting his parents were almost zero.

Almost . . . ?

Why even that small element of doubt? Once she left France she was unlikely to see Griff again. She had to accept that.

Giving Griff an answer to his statement was unnecessary as their main course arrived and their attention was drawn to that.

But that didn't end Sarah's inner curiosity about the couple who had produced this fascinating man. She would have liked nothing better than to meet them one day . . .

But the turn of their conversation had made her wonder, and not for the first time, if it had been Sandra Preston's inability to cope with Griff's profession that had made her cry off the wedding at the last moment like that. Although Griff seemed to be taking an indefinite break away from journalism for the moment, so that didn't exactly add up . . .

And there was no way she could turn around and ask him why his chosen bride had decided not to marry him after all!

Even if she did long to know.

*   *   *

They walked back up to the villa from the restaurant, satisfied with the good food and the equally good company. Although Sarah wasn't so sure she had been that for Griff. But he seemed happy enough, humming softly to himself as they walked along, having placed her hand firmly in the crook of his arm before they'd set out.

He stopped at the top of the driveway to the villa, his hands coming up to cup either side of her face. 'Before we get back I'm going to kiss you goodnight,' he warned. 'I don't want to be accused of taking advantage of the situation.'

Colour heated her cheeks in the dusky darkness, more so because of her earlier apprehension. 'Oh, but——'

'Only joking, Sarah,' he teased softly. 'I know you, and myself, well enough to know there won't be any accusations like that!'

Sarah could see the outline of his face in the moonlight, knew he was going to kiss her, despite the teasing, her lips parting in mute invitation as she raised her face to his.

It was what she had been longing for all day; she knew that as soon as his lips claimed hers, her pulse leaping, excitement coursing through her body, her arms going up about his neck to pull him down to her.

Lights flashed, voices talked in her head——

She looked up dazedly at Griff as he broke the kiss to pull back, his expression unmistakably grim while he looked about them, his whole body tense.

Sarah swallowed hard. 'What is it?' She frowned, turning slightly herself now as the engine of the car they had passed parked on the hill several yards away leapt into life, its light blazing as it sped off down the hill.

'Damn,' Griff muttered between clenched teeth. 'Damn, damn, *damn*! So much for my claim this afternoon that we had time to spend getting to know each other.' He thrust his hands into his trouser pockets. 'Our solitude has been well and truly shattered now. Damn!' He kicked at the stones on the road at his feet.

She shook her head, still puzzled. 'I don't——'

'Did you see the flashing lights just now?' Griff grated impatiently.

Flashing lights . . . and voices talking . . . Was Griff saying that *hadn't* been inside her head?

'It was a camera, Sarah,' he explained hardly, staring frustratedly after the fast-disappearing car. 'Some ba—— The swine took a photograph of us just now as we kissed.' He sighed. 'By tomorrow morning our photograph will be emblazoned on the first page of every rubbish newspaper in England!'

'Where are you, Griff?' they had demanded to know.

And now they knew.

And they also knew *who* he was with.

Oh, God...!

CHAPTER EIGHT

GRIFF made them both coffee once they were inside the villa, both of them fully aware of the publicity that was going to be showered upon them once Griff's whereabouts became public knowledge. Especially as it appeared he had another woman living there with him. After the passionate kiss the camera had captured for all time no one was going to believe they occupied separate bedrooms in the villa!

'How could they have found out where you are?' Sarah said with dismay.

Griff's expression was still grim. 'How indeed?' he drawled slowly. 'Want to lay any bets on this one?' he added heavily.

She frowned up at him in some surprise, her eyes widening as his full implication became clear. 'You can't be serious?' she dismissed. 'Sally couldn't have——'

'I told you that young lady was dangerous,' he rasped. 'And I meant it. I know the type. I'm not fooling myself she actually gives a damn about me, but she's just young enough to think that if she could get you out of the way she might stand a chance with me herself. But she's way out of line with that way of thinking.' He shook his head. 'I don't know, they talk about "a woman scorned", but I think a teenager scorned is much more dangerous!'

Sarah stared at him. 'You talk as if from experience.'

He shrugged. 'Young girls seem to find the slightly risky side to my profession attractive. The need to make me a conquest seems to become doubly important.' He shook his head. 'Maybe some men find that type of attraction—a young girl's for an older man—flattering. I just find it embarrassingly awkward.'

She knew he was right about Sally's infatuation for him being half because of who he was and not the person he was, but even so... 'I can't believe she would inform the Press of your whereabouts,' she dismissed confidently.

Griff's expression softened as he read the puzzled hurt on her face. 'You can be very naïve, Sarah, naïvely sweet,' he added indulgently. 'Perhaps that's why I——' He broke off, straightening briskly. 'I believe we have to make a decision now, and stick to it.' His voice had hardened firmly. 'We either move on elsewhere, separately if that's what you want——' but, from his tone, he obviously didn't '—or we can stay on here, together, and brave it out.' He looked at her challengingly.

Her photograph, with Griff, the two of them kissing each other, emblazoned across English newspapers. It was a horrifying thought, but it was something that was completely out of her hands.

She looked across at Griff hopefully. 'I don't suppose you could... telephone some of the people you know in journalism, and try to— well, get the photograph squashed...? No,' she grimaced as he continued to look at her steadily, almost pityingly, 'I thought not.' She sighed. 'Well, I'll have to telephone my mother and warn her what to expect.'

And Simon—what would he make of her in a passionate clinch with Griff Morgan?

Oh, damn Simon, what did it matter what he thought? He was too busy trying to patch up his marriage to Fiona to give a damn about anyone else!

'My mother isn't going to understand,' she grimaced knowingly, easily able to envisage the difficulty there was going to be explaining this situation to her mother.

'Let me talk to her,' Griff instantly offered.

Sarah's eyes widened. 'You?'

His mouth twisted. 'Believe it or not, I am capable of talking to women your mother's age.'

The trouble was, he could talk to, and charm, women of all ages. Maybe if he weren't so damned attractive none of this would have happened in the first place!

She was being unfair now, and she knew it, but Griff would possibly understand if he knew her mother...

'Be my guest,' she invited. 'But I'm warning you, Clarissa is one of her oldest and dearest friends,' she added as she picked up the receiver and began to dial; it was late to telephone her mother at all, but it had to be better to warn her now what to expect than leaving her to find out for herself in the morning.

'And you're her daughter,' Griff reminded softly.

Sarah grimaced, only half listening to the ring of the telephone against her ear, knowing her mother would already have gone to bed by this time, that it would take her some time to get down the stairs to answer the call. 'She's been a little disappointed already in my behaviour lately.' She shrugged.

'The married man?' Griff dismissed. 'We can all be deceived into believing something is right if we want it badly enough at the time.'

'How——?'

'You wanted someone to love. I wanted someone to love.' He shrugged. 'We just weren't patient enough to wait for the right person to come along for us to love.'

The intensity of his gaze sent a shiver down her spine. 'But——Ah, Mummy.' She spoke into the receiver as her mother at last picked up the telephone her end. 'I know it's late, but—— Everyone is fine,' she assured at her mother's panicked query now that she was fully awake and had realised who her caller was. 'No, I'm still in France. Yes, I——'

'Give it to me,' Griff instructed indulgently as she could only manage to answer her mother's worried questioning, holding out a hand for the receiver.

Sarah looked at him, wondering what he thought he could do any differently to her as her mother continued to gabble on at the other end of the telephone. But surely he couldn't do any worse than she had?

She handed him the receiver.

'Mrs Williams?' His pleasant query obviously had the desired effect, and he winked at Sarah, having her mother's full attention now, quietly but firmly beginning to talk.

It all sounded so straightforward coming from him, Sally's bitchiness over Simon as her initial reason for moving out not even mentioned, the missing bracelet explained in such a way that Griff had to calm her mother's indignation at the unfairness that had been dealt Sarah.

Their own friendship he explained smoothly before coming to the little fact that there would probably be a photograph of the two of them together published the following day, and that it was something they would all just have to get used to, no matter how much they disliked the intrusion.

What he went on to say next made Sarah gasp, her responses made automatically when Griff at last put her back on to her mother.

By the time she'd ended the call she was so angry with Griff that she could have hit him!

She slammed the receiver down, turning on him. 'Well, that was really clever, really helpful,' she stormed. ' "Let me talk to her," ' she mimicked. ' "I am capable of talking to women your mother's age," ' she scorned again. 'You *really* helped the ridiculousness of this situation by telling her we were going to be married!' she blazed, breathing hard as she relived again that mind-numbing moment when he had made that announcement to her mother.

He looked unperturbed. 'She accepted your staying here with me, didn't she?' he dismissed.

'Oh, yes, she——Oh, never mind!' Sarah bit out disgustedly. 'I'm going to bed. I have a headache!'

One *big* headache, and his name was Griff Morgan!

CHAPTER NINE

SARAH didn't want to wake up the next morning, certainly didn't want to get up, burrowing under the bedclothes, wishing the day would just go away and leave her to her misery.

But the sun continued to shine remorselessly through the curtains, and she knew there was no way any of this was going to go away and leave her alone, however much she wanted it to.

But, if she had thought yesterday was bad, how much worse, with that awful photograph imminent, was today going to be?

She had got through before, after Simon, and she would, somehow, have to get through this too. If only Griff hadn't complicated things with her mother. Telling her the two of them were going to be married . . .

She hadn't slept for hours after coming to bed last night, just lying here, going over and over in her mind what it would be like if it were really true. Griff, she felt sure, once committed to the relationship, would make a wonderful husband.

But she wasn't going to be the lucky woman who became his wife.

Rather than still feeling anger towards Sandra Preston, she began to feel pity. The other woman, for all the heartache Griff's career might have given her—for Sarah still couldn't believe there was any other reason why the other woman hadn't gone through with the marriage!—couldn't have known what a wonderful man she'd had in Griff.

Sarah knew, realised how much loyalty Griff had already shown her, unshakeable in his belief in her innocence. He was like one of those heroes in the old-fashioned black and white films she loved so much.

Just her luck to go and find her own real-life hero in the midst of so much chaos in the rest of her life!

She was starting to wonder if happy-ever-after endings really happened ...

She showered quickly, washing her hair to leave it to dry in the warmth of the day, pulling on white shorts and a loose white top, wondering if she had chosen the virginal colour deliberately, and then not caring whether she had or not, the delicious smell of coffee urging her to the kitchen.

She could hear voices in there as she approached, wondering if someone had come over from the neighbouring villa to tell them how the search for the bracelet was going; the flashing camera and then Griff's conversation with her mother had put all thought of telephoning the Forbeses from her mind the night before.

But the two men seated at the breakfast bar with Griff were complete strangers to her, delicate colour staining her cheeks as they both looked across at her curiously.

Griff got up to cross the room to her side, wearing casual trousers and a short-sleeved navy blue shirt. 'Morning, love.' He kissed her lightly on the cheek, his arm going casually about her shoulders as he guided her fully into the room. 'Come and meet two of my ex-colleagues,' he invited lightly, his arm tightening about her slightly as he felt her stiffen next to him. 'I found them skulking in the bushes this morning,' he added confidingly, with a mocking smile in the direction of the two slightly abashed men. 'And, knowing how uncomfortable that can be, I decided it was kinder to invite them in for coffee,' he derided.

The younger of the two men stood up, tall and blond, with a slightly world-weary expression; it was an expression, Sarah had been glad to see, that had been fading from Griff over the last few days, although a little of that hardened veneer was back in the company of these two men.

'Paul Grant,' the blond man introduced himself, thrusting out his hand. 'And this is my photographer, Jim Long.' He slapped the older grey-haired man on the back good-naturedly.

Jim stood up too, smiling ruefully at Sarah's faintly apprehensive expression. 'No, I'm not the one with the camera skulking about in a car last night,' he assured her drily.

He might not be, but he was basically here for the same reason, and Sarah's greeting was strained with both men.

She looked down pointedly to the empty mugs in front of them. 'You're obviously accustomed to the ''Morgan coffee'',' she said wryly.

'Are we ever,' Jim said appreciatively.

'I'll make you a weaker cup, love,' Griff offered, moving slightly away from the group.

'Have you and Griff known each other long?' Paul prompted, eyes narrowed shrewdly.

She shrugged. 'Why don't you ask him that?' She wasn't going to be drawn that easily! 'Excuse me,' she gave them both an over-bright smile, 'I have to go and feed the cat.' She hadn't actually taken on the job of feeding Jasper before, but she didn't particularly want to answer twenty questions while Griff was otherwise occupied either!

Griff gave her a conspiratorial wink as she stood near him, getting the cat food out of the cupboard. 'Trust me,' he murmured for her ears alone. 'I'll deal with these two, and then, hopefully, we won't be bothered again.'

Sarah wished she could be as sure of that!

She caught vague snatches of the conversation as she stood out in the courtyard feeding the cat; 'Lovely girl', and 'don't blame you'; the name Sandra was mentioned, and the word 'wedding', and so Sarah could only assume the conversation was mainly about Griff's public break-up with Sandra Preston. Obviously the other two men would know Sandra as she was the daughter of a newspaper owner, and, from the little Sarah could hear, they were sympathising with Griff over the fact that this lovely girl had walked out on him. Where that left Sarah in their eyes she hated to guess.

'Jim and Paul are leaving now.' Griff stood at the kitchen doorway to tell her. 'And your coffee is getting cold.'

She went back inside reluctantly, making her farewells to the two men politely enough, all the time aware that they were probably comparing her to the beautiful Sandra—and finding Sarah wanting!

When Jim paused before going off in the car to take a photograph of her and Griff together she gave an indignant gasp.

'Leave it,' Griff advised, turning away. 'Hopefully it will be the last.'

She looked at him wordlessly, relaxing slightly as he moved to take her into his arms, his face buried in the silky blonde thickness of her hair, completely dry now from her time spent outside feeding the cat.

'It was the best way, love,' he told her ruefully. 'They have their story now, and their photograph, and they'll go away happy and not bother us any more.'

'With more to follow, I don't doubt.' She shook her head disgustedly at having her privacy invaded in this way.

'Possibly.' Griff moved back, holding her at arm's length. 'But I know how to deal with them, Sarah,' he insisted.

'I'm sure you do,' she accepted wearily, raising a hand to the side of her face. 'But all we need is for one of the Forbes family to speak to one of the reporters and it will be all over the newspapers that you're staying in the south of France with a thief!' She shuddered at the thought of it.

'That's ridiculous,' Griff snapped. 'We know that isn't true.'

'But the great general public don't.' Her voice rose slightly.

'I don't give a damn what anyone else thinks,' he dismissed exasperatedly.

'I do,' Sarah flared. 'You've had a bad enough time this last week without this!'

His expression softened as he realised her concern was only for him. 'I don't care about any of that,' he told her gently. 'I only care about you.'

'Me?' She looked startled. 'But——' She broke off as a knock sounded on the door. 'More reporters, I expect,' she said disgustedly, turning away.

Griff gave a frustrated sigh before going to answer the door.

As Sarah turned away she saw, for the first time, the newspaper that lay on the breakfast bar where the two men had been sitting when she'd joined them earlier. She moved towards it slowly now, sure of what she was going to see before she even did so, guessing that the two men had brought the newspaper over from England with them this morning.

The headline was more or less what she had expected it to be, so there were no points for originality as far as she was concerned! 'There you are, Griff' stood out at the top of the newspaper in three-inch-high black letters.

But the photograph that accompanied the headline had to be the *coup de grâce*—whatever lens and lighting the photographer had had on his camera it had been good, damned good, she and Griff, as they kissed, perfectly visible, completely recognisable.

It was awful!

And it was only the beginning. Admittedly this was one of the more lurid tabloids, the newspaper the two who had just left worked for being slightly more respectable, but, even so, she had a feeling the media as a whole were going to make a meal out of Griff's being here with her.

'A visitor for you, Sarah,' Griff remarked drily from behind her.

She turned with a frown, her eyes widening as she saw Ben standing slightly apart from Griff, the latter having a slightly derisive expression on his face.

Sarah quickly folded the newspaper she still held in half, picture hidden inside, and pushed it to the far end of the breakfast bar.

'Ben,' she greeted half questioningly. 'What a surprise.'

He shot an awkward glance at Griff, his hands thrust into the pockets of his denims. 'I thought I would come over and see how you are,' he muttered, giving the other man a resentful glare.

'Well, as you can see,' Griff moved to lean against one of the kitchen units, 'she's fine.'

'As I can see . . .' Ben mumbled. 'I just——' He broke off as the telephone began to ring in the lounge.

Griff straightened, frowning. 'Damn thing's been ringing all morning,' he muttered before striding off to answer the call.

Ben visibly relaxed once they were alone, smiling encouragingly at Sarah. 'How are you really?'

'I'm really fine,' she lightly mocked. 'How is the search for the bracelet going?' She sobered.

He shrugged. 'It hasn't turned up yet.'

That didn't really come as any surprise to Sarah, not after what Griff had said about it, but that didn't stop her feeling disappointed none the less.

'But it will,' Ben added confidently. 'Why don't you come back and stay at the villa with us and we could look for the bracelet together? We're sure to find it.'

Sarah looked at him sharply, his tone sounding a little too confident. How could he possibly be so sure——? My God, it couldn't have been *Ben* who'd taken the bracelet, after all?

She frowned at him in growing disbelief. He couldn't have taken the bracelet—what possible reason could he have for doing something like that to her?

Unbidden, a memory of the malevolent resentment on Ben's face the day he had escorted his mother out for the evening, because he was absolutely furious over the time she had spent with Griff that afternoon, came to mind.

The bracelet had gone missing from Clarissa's jewellery box after Sarah had walked out over the upset with Sally, to spend the night here with Griff, albeit innocently...

Ben seemed to become aware of the slowly dawning horror on her face, avoiding her gaze. 'Well, I only came over to see how you were,' he excused, turning to leave.

'Ben!'

Her resolve weakened as he looked back at her, suddenly knowing, with sickening clarity, that she was right in her suspicion; Ben was at the root of this latest heartache.

She let him leave.

What had she ever really done to him, except find him too young for her to be attracted to?

But she realised now that he had taken her initial friendliness as encouragement to believe she was attracted to him, that his ego must more than match his mother's and sister's.

Griff was right—poor Roger; he was a lamb among savage lions!

But Sarah knew now what she had to do.

'More reporters,' Griff muttered as he finally came back from answering the telephone call.

'It must make a change, being on the receiving end,' Sarah remarked vaguely.

He grimaced. 'If I hadn't already decided to have a break from journalism myself this would have been enough to make me decide to do so! The personal questions some of them ask...!' He shook his head. 'No Ben?' He suddenly realised their visitor had gone.

'No. He——' she looked away, still stunned by the discovery she had made '—he only came over to tell me they haven't found the bracelet yet.'

Griff's mouth twisted. 'Wanted to be the bearer of the "good news", did he?'

She shrugged. 'I forgot to telephone them last night.'

'Sarah,' he sighed, 'we both know that bracelet isn't going to turn up until Sally is ready for it to do so.'

She swallowed hard, chewing on her bottom lip. 'I have a feeling you're wrong about our culprit, Griff,' she told him huskily.

'I'm sure——' He broke off at the steady certainty in her gaze, looking at her face searchingly. 'Ben?' he finally realised doubtfully. 'What makes you think it was him?'

She moved restlessly about the room. 'It was something about his manner, a certainty that the bracelet would eventually turn up, especially if

I returned to the villa with him. And he didn't imply that *I* was the one who was going to suddenly find it, but at the same time he seemed to know the bracelet hadn't gone permanently missing.'

'He could also be like that if he knew his sister had removed it out of spite,' Griff pointed out reasoningly.

Sarah sighed. 'I suppose so—I just feel that it was Ben.'

Griff looked at the paleness of her cheeks, the pain in her eyes, her discovery all the more disillusioning because she had believed Ben to be her friend.

'I believe you.' Griff finally nodded. 'The question is, what are we going to do about it?'

'*We* aren't going to do anything,' she told him drily. '*I'm* going over there to confront him with it.'

'I'm coming with you,' Griff told her decisively.

'No,' she answered as firmly. 'I have to do this alone.'

'Why didn't you just accuse him of it while he was here?' Griff frowned.

'The truth?' She gave a rueful smile. 'Because I think he is more likely to admit to it away from you!'

'Me?' Griff looked incredulous. 'Why would he——? Ah,' he nodded, understanding, 'he thinks I'm likely to beat him to a pulp if he admits to being the one to hurt you? He's right, of course,' he added grimly.

'Which is why I'm going over to their villa alone to sort out this situation once and for all.' She nodded.

'Now?' he protested.

Sarah arched blonde brows. 'There's no time like the present.'

'But we have so much to talk about ourselves, Sarah,' he reasoned.

The pain and disillusionment they had both shared. But, most of all, that ridiculous announcement he had made to her mother!

'There's so much we have to say to each other,' he pushed at her hesitation.

'It will have to wait, Griff.' She straightened decisively. 'I need to remove the shadows from my life, one at a time, before I can even think about what we have to say to each other. And

Ben and the missing bracelet are the start of them,' she said firmly.

'But you——' He broke off with an angry sigh as the ringing of the telephone interrupted them yet again. 'I'll have that damned thing disconnected!' He scowled as he strode off into the adjoining room once more.

Sarah could hear his voice seconds later as he picked up the receiver, his tone aggressive, to say the least.

He was right; the two of them did have to talk, but it would have to wait for a while.

She followed him through to the dining-room, where the telephone was, intending to wait patiently while he finished the call before making her excuses and going over to the neighbouring villa.

'I wouldn't do that, Sandra,' he was advising softly. 'That's how *you* saw our relationship,' he answered another of the woman's comments. 'I always saw it as something completely different. Yes, I know...'

Sarah didn't listen to any more of the conversation, hurrying from the room, her cheeks blazing.

Sandra!

And the other woman had telephoned Griff here, just as soon as she had found out from the newspapers where he was.

That could only mean one thing.

Sandra wanted Griff back . . .

CHAPTER TEN

'It's just a ploy, Roger,' Clarissa dismissed indignantly. 'To get herself out of trouble. It has to be!'

Sarah had found the two older Forbeses inside the villa preparing lunch together when she'd arrived a short time ago, imagining that the children were down by the pool. Clarissa had been very reluctant to hear what she had to say, although Roger had insisted she be given a fair hearing.

But even he looked slightly disbelieving at her claim that Ben had taken the bracelet, and his reason for it.

Not that Sarah could exactly blame Roger. If it was true it meant he had a lot of straightening out to do with both his older children—Stephen, too, if the way he was growing into such a little monster was anything to go by. Sarah didn't envy Roger his problems, but she needed to have her name cleared once and for all.

'I'm not in trouble, Clarissa.' She turned to the other woman, talking with more confidence than she actually felt—if this couple eventually decided to go to the police she could find herself in a lot of trouble indeed! 'You see,' she added challengingly, 'I *know* I'm innocent, and I think, if the two of you are completely honest, you know I am too.'

Roger sighed. 'I've never for a moment believed in your guilt, but the——'

'Roger!' Clarissa protested exasperatedly.

'—alternative is even more unpalatable,' Roger concluded heavily.

'There is no alternative,' Clarissa told them both firmly, two bright spots of colour in her cheeks. 'Sarah has to be the one who removed my bracelet.'

'Have I?' she prompted quietly.

'Of course you have.' The other woman was becoming very agitated in the face of Sarah's calm confidence. 'Even if it were true that Ben has become infatuated with you——'

'I would say it was true.' Roger nodded consideringly.

Clarissa gave him an impatient glare. 'Then you must have encouraged him,' she accused Sarah. 'You seem to have this need to make every male you come into contact with fall in love with you. Look at you now, living with a man you haven't even known a week!' she accused triumphantly, as if that had to prove that the other accusation was true too.

Sarah felt as if she had known Griff for a lifetime, was a little dazed herself to realise Clarissa was right, and it was in fact, only a few days since she had first met him.

She couldn't help wondering if Griff and Sandra would have sorted out their differences via the telephone by the time she got back. Were they even now discussing a new wedding date? She felt an ache in her chest at the thought of it.

'She is hardly living with the man, Clarissa,' Roger dismissed. 'We made it impossible for her to stay here!'

'But——'

'I'm going to look in Ben's bedroom,' he told his wife firmly.

'You can't do that!' she protested.

He took hold of Clarissa by the shoulders, shaking her gently. 'The other night I told you I wanted this family sorted out once and for all,' he reminded softly. 'And that meant especially the children. They have all grown up to be selfish little monsters, and if it turns out Ben has taken your bracelet to incriminate Sarah...! You do realise Sarah could press charges? That she will have been wrongfully accused?' he prompted gently.

Clarissa turned to Sarah with widely apprehensive eyes.

And that was when Sarah knew that Clarissa half believed her claim despite her protestations to the contrary.

This was more or less confirmed for her when the two women sat and waited for Roger in complete silence, Clarissa's movements agitated as she kept glancing at the door, waiting for Roger's return.

A white-faced Roger came back from Ben's bedroom a short time later, the gold and diamond bracelet dangling between limp fingers.

As soon as Clarissa saw the bracelet she sprang to her feet with a choked cry, staring at the gaudy piece of jewellery as if she wished she never had to see it again.

Sarah felt sure the other woman would never wear the bracelet again...

'It was hidden under the mattress of his bed,' Roger told them shakily. 'Not very original,' he choked. 'But then, I don't suppose he ever thought we would search *his* room for it.' He shook his head dazedly.

'Oh, Roger,' Clarissa moved into his arms, 'what are we going to do?'

'I don't——'

'Sarah!' Ben came in through the open french doors from the garden, his face alight with pleasure at seeing her there. 'Have you changed your mind and come back after all? I didn't think——' He broke off as his father wordlessly held up the glittering bracelet, Ben realising for the first time that they were all looking at him with varying degrees of dismay.

Strangely, Sarah knew she was the one who felt the least upset now that it was all over; after all, Ben was Clarissa's and Roger's son, and they would have to cope with his personality problems on a day to day basis from now on; *she* had just wanted her name cleared.

While she watched Ben's face as it went from white to grey she knew she had done that.

'Ben——'

'You had no right going into my bedroom and looking through my things.' He turned viciously on his father.

'Ben, you've committed a crime——'

'What crime?' he challenged. 'I only removed my mother's bracelet to my room for a few days.'

Roger nodded. 'At the same time implicating Sarah.'

'And why not?' Ben's voice rose. 'She wouldn't go out with me, treated me like a child. And then Griff Morgan came along and she didn't even seem to notice I was alive any more. I thought if I took the bracelet she would turn to me for support. And instead of that she went with *him*,' he bit out between clenched teeth. 'I only wanted——'

'I think,' Sarah cut in softly, her hands clenched into fists at her sides at this young man's warped attempt to make her emotionally dependent on him if he couldn't get her to be attracted to him in the normal way, 'that it's past time, Ben, when you learnt you can't have everything you want. No matter how hard you plot and scheme for it.' She frowned at the lengths he had been prepared to go to.

'I only wanted you to like me——'

'I do like you—or, at least, I did,' she amended heavily. 'I would never trust you with my friendship again. And that's all I would ever have felt towards you, no matter what you might have done to make it more.' She sighed. 'And now I think I had better leave. But please take my advice,' she pleaded with Clarissa and Roger. 'For all your sakes!'

She had reached the front door before Clarissa caught up with her, and she turned defensively to face the other woman, waiting for the verbal blows to fall. At least she was ready for them!

Clarissa gave a rueful grimace, pale beneath her tan. 'I can't blame you for thinking I've followed you out here to hurl more abuse at you.' Her voice was huskily soft. 'I actually wanted to say how sorry I am. For everything.'

Sarah certainly wasn't ready for *this*!

She stared at the other woman wordlessly, knowing what the apology had cost Clarissa by the strain about her eyes and mouth; she suddenly looked older than her forty-three years.

Clarissa gave a self-derisive smile that contained no humour, only pain. 'Roger and I had the most terrible argument the other night after you left,' she revealed gruffly. 'He told me he was on the point of leaving me, that there was no one else involved, certainly not you——'

'I'm certainly not!' Sarah gasped, as shocked by Roger's admission as Clarissa must have been; he had always seemed so much in love with his wife.

'I knew that.' Clarissa squeezed her arm reassuringly. 'Roger has always loved me, only me, and . . . I know it's no excuse for the selfish bitch I'm become—but I suppose I've become complacent in that love, taken so many things for granted as I went my own selfish way, including Roger. But,' her mouth twisted self-derisively, 'the worm finally turned two days ago. And I realised he really meant what he said,' she added bleakly. 'That Roger might still love me, but that he could no longer live with the selfish bitch I've become over the years.' She swallowed hard. 'It's only when you realise you might lose something you've taken so much for granted that you come to know how much it means to you. Without Roger my life would be nothing,' she admitted with simple honesty. 'We still have a long way to go, and I realise you might have thought just now was me acting with my usual bitchiness, but I hope you'll realise I was simply a lioness trying to protect one of my cubs.'

Clarissa was more like the leopard trying to change its spots overnight. But Sarah realised as she thought over the woman's behaviour today,

Clarissa was at least trying. And maybe this softer, more vulnerable side to Clarissa was the one her mother knew and felt such affection for. Sarah hoped so.

She knew she and Clarissa would never become close friends themselves, that the two of them were too different, that they had no common interests, but she certainly didn't wish the other woman any harm, sincerely hoped the problems of her marriage could be sorted out.

But, given the problems this couple had with both Sally and Ben, it was going to be an uphill struggle!

'It will work out.' Clarissa accurately read Sarah's doubts from her expression, smiling ruefully, some of the colour starting to return to her cheeks now.

Looking at the firm resolve in the other woman's face, Sarah couldn't help but believe it would too!

Clarissa leant forward impulsively, kissing Sarah warmly on the cheek. 'Margaret should be very proud of you,' she said wistfully. 'I would be if you were my daughter. And I hope you find your happiness with Griff.'

Sarah had been recovering slowly from the real affection she sensed in the other woman's kiss, but Clarissa's remark about Griff sobered her instantly, reminding her all too forcefully that Griff had been talking to Sandra as she'd left him earlier.

'I had better go,' she said abruptly. 'I really wish all of you well.'

'I know you do.' Clarissa nodded. 'Say goodbye to Griff for us.'

Sarah could be saying goodbye to him herself in the very near future—there was no longer any reason for her to stay on in the south of France!

Except that she loved Griff...

And by now he could have patched up his differences with Sandra, might even now be packing to go to the other woman. They would probably be returning to England on the same plane—Griff to Sandra, she to the loneliness of loving Griff herself.

She didn't want to go back to the villa to find that out just yet, deciding to go for a long walk instead, putting off the dreaded moment for as long as possible.

When the drops of summer rain began to fall on her bare arms she knew she would have to go back, knew from experience that there would be quite a shower before it was warm and sunny once again. In the meantime she would get soaked.

There was a red car that she hadn't seen before parked next to Griff's outside the villa. Yet more reporters, Sarah would hazard a guess.

But at least if he had visitors Griff couldn't have already left!

She had only time to let herself in and walk into the hallway, turning to close the door behind her, when Griff burst out of the lounge, his expression one of barely controlled fury.

'Where the hell have you been?' he demanded without preamble.

'I——'

'You disappeared from here this morning without even saying goodbye, and I know you left the Forbeses over an hour ago, because I called them,' he accused. 'So where have you been?'

'I——' Sarah gasped, her eyes wide.

For standing in the doorway behind Griff, totally recognisable from the original photograph of her Sarah had seen in the newspaper, was Sandra Preston!

CHAPTER ELEVEN

SARAH'S first thought, ridiculously, was that this woman must have been telephoning Griff from the airport this morning to have got here so quickly after talking to him.

She turned back to Griff, trying to read from his expression how the other woman's visit had affected him. But he was still glaring angrily at Sarah, so it was difficult to tell!

'Stop bullying the poor girl, Griff,' Sandra Preston drawled, moving forward to tuck her hand cosily into the crook of Griff's arm.

They looked so much an established couple like that, Sarah realised achingly.

Sandra had the naturally tanned skin that often went with that particular shade of ash-blonde hair, her eyes so deep a blue that they looked almost violet, looking tall and slender in the fitted yellow sundress.

With a start of surprise Sarah realised the other woman had a huge diamond engagement ring on her left hand. Griff's ring...?

Sarah straightened, meeting Griff's gaze without flinching. 'You were busy talking on the telephone when I left this morning.' The pointed look she gave the other woman told him she knew exactly who he had been talking to too. 'I had already told you I was going to see the Forbeses to straighten things out. I've done that,' she added flatly, 'but I needed to go for a walk afterwards,' as much to get the nasty taste from her mouth as not returning back to see Griff straight away.

His eyes were narrowed. 'You were right about Ben?'

'Yes,' she confirmed abruptly. 'As I said, it's all sorted out. And now I'm sorry for interrupting the two of you. I'll just go and——'

'You didn't interrupt anything,' Griff rasped, disentangling himself from Sandra Preston's clinging hand to cross to Sarah's side and lightly clasp her arms. 'Are you all right?' he probed gently.

She was going to be. One day. When she got over loving this man.

If she ever did...

'Yes,' she dismissed briskly, looking uncomfortably over his shoulder at Sandra Preston, surprising a venomous glitter in the other woman's eyes. 'I'm sure you and Sandra have a lot to talk about,' she excused again, the smile she attempted turning out brittle, but it was the best she could do in the circumstances.

'Actually, we have very little to say to each other,' Griff dismissed, turning to face Sandra now, his arm slipping easily about Sarah's shoulders. 'In fact, I think nothing at all,' he challenged.

The other woman looked disconcerted for a few seconds, but that look was quickly replaced by a teasing smile. 'I know you're a little cross with me at the moment, Griff.' She pouted as he gave a disbelieving snort, the pout a little childish on a woman who must be thirty, possibly a little older; somehow, from the photograph Sarah had seen of her, she had expected Sandra to be younger than that, but, close to like this, she could see that she wasn't. 'But I've said I'm sorry.' She looked at him appealingly with wide violet-coloured eyes. 'I don't see what the problems are to our sorting things out between us.'

His mouth twisted. 'Apart from the basic ones, which I've already made perfectly clear,' he ground out, 'there is one other big problem.' His arm tightened about Sarah's shoulders, and he looked down at her warmly.

Sarah couldn't exactly blame him for using her as an emotional shield; he had very recently been badly hurt and humiliated by this woman. And she, Sarah, did owe him for all the help he had given her. But he could badly regret being this cruel to Sandra once he had thought this through sensibly; the other woman had obviously changed her mind and wanted him back, and revenge for hurt pride wasn't worth losing her again, surely?

'You're just being ridiculous about this, Griff,' Sandra snapped irritably. 'You don't even know this girl.'

Girl? She was probably seven or eight years younger than the other woman, but even so...

'That's where you are totally wrong,' Griff drawled. 'I knew her the moment I met her.'

'But——'

'It's over between us, Sandra,' he continued coldly. 'I'm going to marry Sarah.'

Sarah looked up at him sharply. 'I wish you would stop——'

'Do you really want a rebound love?' The other woman looked at her scathingly. 'Never knowing whether Griff only wanted you as a salve to his injured pride? Never quite sure how long he's going to stay——?'

'That's enough, Sandra,' Griff cut in harshly. 'When I marry Sarah it will be forever.'

Sandra's mouth firmed into an ugly scarlet gash. 'You'll regret this!'

He looked down at Sarah. 'I don't think so,' he said confidently.

Sandra turned briefly and picked up the yellow clutch-bag that perfectly matched the colour of her dress. 'My father will see that you suffer for this,' she spat out, all outward signs of the repentant fiancée gone in her anger.

Griff looked at her pityingly. 'I don't think so—your father is a gentleman.'

She wrenched the engagement ring off her finger. 'I should have given you this back last time!' She thrust the ring into Griff's hand. 'Maybe your little innocent would like it,' she added insultingly.

'You chose this monstrosity,' Griff bit out, looking down at the diamond ring with distaste, 'you may as well keep it.' He took her clutch-bag, opened it, and dropped the ring inside before pushing the bag back into Sandra's hand. 'Keep it as a reminder of our lucky escape.'

'Why, you——!' Her hand was stopped from making contact with his face as Griff easily grasped her wrist. 'You're a fool, Griff Morgan,' she scorned as she wrenched free of him. 'We could have had a good marriage, had tremendous fun together, and instead you want to settle down in Suburbia with a little secretary——'

'Sarah is a nurse, actually,' he cut in mockingly. 'And the sort of fun you're talking about I can do without!'

Sandra gave Sarah a scathing glance. 'I think you're going to have to!'

Sarah felt a warm colour in her cheeks. Really, she had been insulted by experts during this time in Francc. And most of it undeservedly.

She could quite easily understand Griff's hurt pride, but did he have to keep telling people they were getting married? He was going to look very foolish when they didn't!

Sandra looked at them both coldly. 'What an utterly boring couple you're going to make,' was her parting shot, the door slamming loudly behind her.

'Whew.' Griff relaxed slightly, his arm falling away from Sarah's shoulders. 'What a lifesaver you are, Sarah.' He gave a strained grin. 'I thought I was never going to get rid of her.'

Nice to know she was good for something!

'I'm going to get my things together now,' she told him dully. 'And then I'm going to telephone the airport and see if I can get a flight home.'

'It's already done,' Griff told her cheerfully. 'I made the booking this morning.'

Sarah looked at him with widely hurt eyes; he couldn't wait to get rid of her now, could he?

'For both of us,' he added, instantly dismissing her theory.

'You're going back to England too?' She frowned. 'But I thought you came here to work.'

'We both know that wasn't my initial reason for coming here,' he drawled. 'And the book can wait a week or two longer, as it's already waited this long. There are some things I have to clear up in England before coming back here.'

'Oh. I see.' Sarah nodded dully, all her hopes finally dashed; he was going back because he had business in England; it was pure coincidence that he was returning with her.

'I doubt it,' he drawled. 'But you will.'

That sounded a little ominous, but Sarah could read nothing from his expression as he just grinned at her conspiratorially and refused to be drawn any further.

Travelling with Griff was even more hectic than travelling with the Forbes tribe had been!

Somehow several more of Griff's ex-colleagues had managed to find out which flight they were on, and they were mobbed by reporters as soon as they left Customs at Heathrow Airport.

The flight over itself had been made worse by the fact that Sandra had been on the same flight as them, returning to England herself, her trip to France having been a wasted one. It was a possibility that neither Griff nor Sarah had thought of!

Although it turned out to be lucky for them once the reporters realised who Sandra was, all rushing off to interview her, their curiosity in full flow.

'Your address?' Griff prompted Sarah as they managed to get into a waiting taxi.

Sarah gave it to him distractedly, knowing the time had come for them to part. On the drive down to Nice, even on the flight over, she had been able to put such thoughts from her mind, but now she realised it was only half an hour or so until they parted, probably never to meet again.

That was why she was surprised when Griff paid the taxi fare and got out on to the pavement beside her.

'Do you live around here too?' She looked at him incredulously once they were alone; it would be too ironic if they had only lived around the corner from each other all the time!

'I do now,' he grinned. 'How big is your flat?'

'My——? Griff, you can't stay with me,' she protested as she realised what he was implying.

He picked up both their suitcases. 'Where else would I stay but with my wife?'

'Griff, I'm not——'

'But you will be,' he said confidently, looking up admiringly at the Victorian building where she had her flat. 'How many bedrooms do you have?' He began to walk up the steps to the main door.

'One.' Sarah stumbled after him. 'But——'

'It will do,' he nodded. 'As a start. We'll have to move eventually, of course, but——'

'Griff, will you stop this now?' She felt like stamping her foot in frustration at this ability he had to listen only to what he wanted to hear. And at the moment he wasn't making the slightest bit of sense! 'There's no one you need protect yourself from here, Griff,' she reasoned gently as he turned to look at her. 'And the more people you tell we're getting married the worse it will be when we don't.'

He put the suitcases down on the top step, his arms folded challengingly across the front of his chest. 'I'm not taking no for an answer,' he told her stubbornly. 'Even if I have to camp out on your doorstep until you say yes!'

'Griff, why are you doing this?' she groaned, her face pale.

'Why?' he repeated incredulously. 'Because I love you, you silly woman.'

Sarah could only gaze at him for several stunned seconds, and then she shook her head sadly. 'You can't——'

'Love you?' he finished questioningly. 'Of course I can,' he dismissed impatiently. 'You're everything that any man in his right mind could love.'

'An innocent.' She made that sound as insulting as Sandra Preston had earlier. 'Suburban. Secretary material. *Boring.*' She clearly remembered all of the barbs, because all of them had struck home, perfectly illustrating her unsuitability for Griff, her lack of attraction for him.

He grinned at her unconcernedly as he wrapped his arms about her and gathered her to him. 'Delightful. Fun. Loyal. Patient. Enchantingly lovely. Sexy,' he added huskily.

'Griff——'

'Do you think we could move off this step away from prying eyes?' he murmured against her throat as he nibbled his way down its creamy length.

The only spectator that Sarah could see was a rather bored-looking black and white cat, which she knew belonged to one of her neighbours, sitting at the bottom of the steps.

'OK, so I just want the chance to get you alone.' Griff grinned down at her. 'I admit it.'

Considering that they had actually been living alone together at the villa in France, Sarah knew he was only teasing her. But going up to the privacy of her flat might not be a bad idea; it seemed they still had a lot to discuss.

She could see that Griff liked her décor, the scatter rugs on the floor, huge brightly coloured cushions too, more rugs of different colours and shapes adorning the walls instead of pictures, the only piece of furniture in the room a huge old-fashioned sofa that had seen better days but which Sarah had seen in a junk shop and re-covered, and revarnished the Victorian-style woodwork on the legs and arms.

It was to this that Griff went, pushing the cushions up and down, as if testing their comfort. He grinned as he saw her watching him curiously. 'It will do.' He nodded. 'For me to sleep on,' he added as she still looked puzzled. 'Until after we're married.' He dropped down on to the plump cushions. 'I hope you don't think it's too old-fashioned of me, but I would rather wait until our wedding-night before we make love.'

'Griff——'

'Come on,' he jumped lightly to his feet, 'dump your things in your bedroom and let's get going.'

He was going too fast for her, much too fast!

'Where?' She frowned dazedly.

'Unfinished business to clear up,' he reminded.

She sighed. 'You don't need me for that.'

'Of course I do,' he said teasingly. 'It's no good going to see him on my own, is it?'

Sarah put up a weary hand over her eyes. 'Griff, it's been a long day, and I'm tired, and——'

'Once this particular piece of business has been dealt with we can relax. I promise.' He held up his hands defensively. 'Then I can just spend my time seducing you into loving me.'

She didn't need seducing for *that*! Didn't he know, hadn't he realised yet, that she already loved him?

'Griff, I really would rather stay here while you go off and see this business colleague on your own,' she sighed, suddenly feeling very tired indeed.

He sobered, moving to lightly touch her shoulders. 'I'm not going to see a business colleague——'

She shook her head. 'Whoever——?'

'Simon, I think you once told me his name is.' He frowned.

'*Simon?*' She stiffened defensively. 'Why on earth should I want to go and see Simon? Why should *you*?'

'So that you can see once and for all that you don't love him, that you never did,' Griff told her gently. 'You couldn't respond to me the way you do, the person I *know* you are couldn't,' he insisted, 'if you were in love with another man.'

Sarah shook her head exasperatedly. 'Of course I don't love him!' she agreed. 'And no, I don't think I ever did.' Because loving Griff had made anything she had ever felt for any other man pale into insignificance. 'I don't need to see him again to know that,' she said with certainty.

'But——'

'Griff, I love you,' she cut in impatiently; there—she had said it!

He stared at her for several seconds, searching into the very depth of her. '*I* thought you did,' he finally murmured. 'I just didn't think you had realised it yet.'

'Well, I have,' she bit out, so tense now that she felt as if she might break in half.

'You know I was talking to Paul and Jim this morning?' Griff seemed hesitant.

She frowned. 'Of course I do.'

'Well, I told them I was going to marry you too,' he revealed with a rueful grimace.

'Griff!' She groaned her dismay, easily able to envisage the newspaper headlines in the morning; no wonder the two men had gone away happy. And she had completely misunderstood, obviously, the parts of that conversation she had overheard . . .

He looked at her with teasing affection. 'Love me?'

'Very much.' She began to smile ruefully.

He held out his arms to her. 'Then what are we going to do about it?'

She gave a choked laugh as she moved unhesitantly into his welcoming arms.

Griff loved her . . .

'I have a confession to make,' he told her a long time later, the two of them entwined on the sofa, Sarah's cheeks flushed from the intensity of their kisses.

She no longer doubted that he loved her!

'Another one?' She looked up at him, not in the least alarmed this time, knowing she trusted this man implicitly.

He grimaced, lightly kissing her on the lips before continuing. 'You know I've told you that things aren't always what they seem?'

'Repeatedly,' she derided affectionately, reaching up to wipe off some of her lip-gloss from his cheek.

He drew in a deep breath. 'I wasn't stood up at the altar by Sandra. Oh, I know I waited at the church and she didn't arrive,' he conceded at Sarah's disbelieving look. 'But the thing is, I knew she wasn't going to arrive.' He frowned. 'It had been pre-arranged that she wouldn't.'

Sarah frowned. 'But——'

'I was the one who broke off our engagement,' Griff sighed. 'When Sandra and I first met it was at a time in my life when I felt I had to put down roots, have somewhere, someone to come back to, a family. Sandra's reasons for accepting my proposal were just as wrong. She liked the idea of being married to someone who was relatively well-known,' he dismissed his own importance, 'was away a lot, and so enabling her to continue with the social life she enjoyed so much, someone who was basically not too demanding of her time. We were both at fault,' he accepted. 'Because we were both willing to settle for second best.' The way his arms tightened about Sarah told her that he now knew what—and who—the 'best' was.

'What happened to change that?' Sarah prompted, realising that something must have done, something had provoked the events of the last week.

He shrugged. 'I'd had enough of running around the world chasing stories, decided I would like to give all that up and write a book. Sandra was furious at the idea of the lost prestige, having a husband constantly under her feet, getting in the way of "friendships" she seemed to feel she wanted to continue after we were married. That was when I realised that the thought of being around Sandra all the time was a horrifying one for me too! I was trying to find a way to tactfully break the engagement when Sandra went running to her father and got him to refuse to release me from my contract.' His face was grim at the memory. 'I'm afraid I was no longer interested in being tactful after that— I just wanted out . . . of reporting and my commitment to Sandra. David, her father, could see how determined I was, and he . . . he came up with the idea that I could save Sandra the humiliation of being jilted, and in return he would release me from my contract.'

A gentlemen's agreement, Sarah realised.

'What about your humiliation?' she said indignantly. As far as she was concerned, Sandra Preston was a spoilt little madam.

He gave a rueful shrug. 'I would go through it all again if I knew I was going to meet you two days later!'

Sarah frowned. 'I wondered why, if you loved her, you hadn't chased after Sandra.'

His arms tightened about her. 'Just *you* try it and see what happens.'

'I won't,' she said with certainty. 'I love you very much, Griff.' She touched his cheek gently.

'And I love you, the future Mrs Morgan.' He kissed her lingeringly on the lips.

She smiled up at him lovingly. 'As long as I don't have to drink the "Morgan coffee" too often.'

'I promise,' he grinned.

She sobered, suddenly biting her bottom lip. 'I still haven't told you about Simon.'

'Tell me later,' Griff prompted, his mouth travelling a slow, nerve-tingling path to her lips. 'Much later.'

If she could even think straight later!

Sarah turned to smile at Griff as he came down the steps to join her by the pool. 'How's it going, darling?' She held out her hand to him, quivering slightly as he began to kiss her fingertips.

'Finished,' he announced with satisfaction. 'Now all we have to do is send it to the publisher and wait for his reaction.'

She felt sure it would be a favourable one. Griff had sent the first couple of chapters of his novel to a publisher several months ago, and they had been very interested in taking the completed manuscript.

Sarah had read all of it but the last few pages he had just completed, and knew it was good. Griff's new career was firmly launched she was sure.

They had been married six months now, and Sarah still had to pinch herself each morning to make sure she wasn't dreaming she was lying next to the man she loved and who undoubtedly loved her.

Griff sat down on the lounger next to hers, her hand still in his, their fingers interlaced. He looked about them appreciatively. 'I must say, it was very convenient of Virginia to fall in love with Richard on her cruise and decide to marry and move to England with him,' he drawled teasingly.

They both knew it wasn't 'convenient' at all, that Virginia had met Richard, a widower in his fifties, and the two of them had genuinely fallen in love.

Sarah had got to know her sister-in-law very well the last six months, had found that beneath the cool exterior she was a very warm and generous woman, truly fond of her only sibling.

She had met Griff's parents too, had found them to be everything Griff had said they were. They were also warm and charming, and had welcomed her into their family like another daughter.

Virginia had sold the villa in the south of France to them as she'd no longer needed it, and they had moved here three months ago, and Griff had been working constantly on his book since then. Sarah was taking some time off from nursing, although she hoped to be able to return to it soon. Her mother had been out to see them for a short visit last month, and, although Sarah hadn't wanted to ask directly how the Forbes family were doing, her mother had casually told her that the family was all still together. Even that had to be indicative of a certain amount of success on Clarissa's and Roger's part.

'How about celebrating the finished manuscript?' Griff said now suggestively.

She deliberately pretended to misunderstand him. 'I suppose we could make arrangements to go out to dinner——Griff!' She laughed her protest as he stood up, taking her with him.

'I had an idea to do our celebrating at home,' he told her wickedly, swinging her up into his arms.

'Why, Griff Morgan!' She pretended shocked outrage.

'Yes—Sarah Morgan?' He was striding purposefully towards the villa.

'Nothing.' She snuggled against him, her arms about his neck. 'Absolutely nothing.'

Happiness was in loving this man, and in being loved by him in return.

She was happy.

**Relive the romance...
Harlequin and Silhouette
are proud to present**

by Request

A program of collections of three complete novels by the most requested authors with the most requested themes. Be sure to look for one volume each month with three complete novels by top name authors.

In June: **NINE MONTHS** Penny Jordan
                                          Stella Cameron
                                          Janice Kaiser

Three women pregnant and alone. But a lot can happen in nine months!

In July: **DADDY'S HOME**   Kristin James
                                          Naomi Horton
                                          Mary Lynn Baxter

Daddy's Home... and his presence is long overdue!

In August: **FORGOTTEN PAST**   Barbara Kaye
                                          Pamela Browning
                                          Nancy Martin

Do you dare to create a future if you've forgotten the past?

Available at your favorite retail outlet.

HARLEQUIN®   Silhouette

New York Times Bestselling Author

Sandra Brown

Tomorrow's Promise

**She cherished the memory
of love but was consumed
by a new passion too
fierce to ignore.**

For Keely Preston, the memory of her husband
Mark has been frozen in time since the day he was
listed as missing in action. And now, twelve years
later, twenty-six men listed as MIA have been
found.

Keely's torn between hope for Mark and despair
for herself. Because now, after all the years of
waiting, she has met another man!

**Don't miss TOMORROW'S PROMISE by
SANDRA BROWN.**

**Available in June wherever Harlequin
books are sold.**